Gabby DURAN

and the Unsittables

ELISE ALLEN & DARYLE CONNERS

Disney • HYPERION

LOS ANGELES   NEW YORK

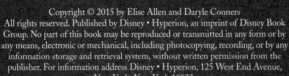

First Hardcover Edition, May 2015
1 3 5 7 9 10 8 6 4 2
G475-5664-5-15046
Printed in the United States of America
This book is set in Adobe Caslon Pro
Designed by Marci Senders
Reinforced binding
Library of Congress Cataloging-in-Publication Data
Allen, Elise, author.
   Gabby Duran and the Unsittables / Elise Allen & Daryle Conners.—First edition.
      pages cm
   Summary: Twelve-year-old Gabby is recruited by a secret agency to take care of
extraterrestrial children.
   ISBN 978-1-4847-0935-1
   [1. Extraterrestrial beings—Fiction. 2. Babysitters—Fiction. 3. Spies—Fiction.
4. Middle schools—Fiction. 5. Schools—Fiction.] I. Conners, Daryle, author. II.
Title.
   PZ7.A42558Gab 2015
   [Fic]—dc23   2014029945

Visit www.DisneyBooks.com

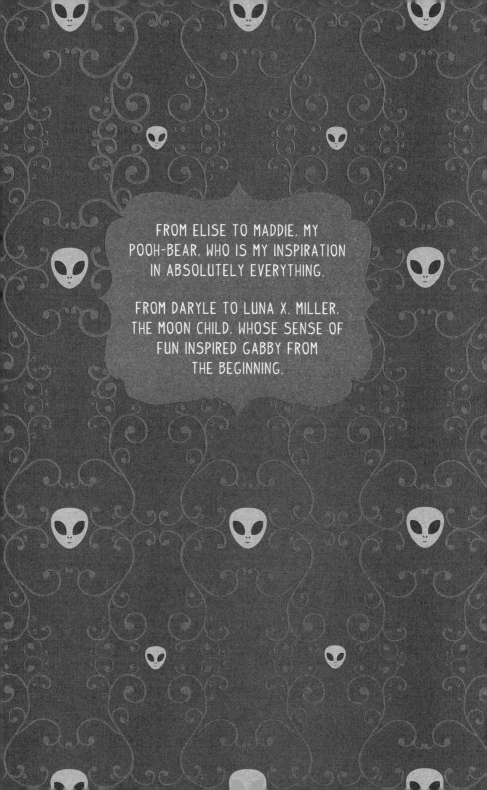

FROM ELISE TO MADDIE, MY
POOH-BEAR, WHO IS MY INSPIRATION
IN ABSOLUTELY EVERYTHING.

FROM DARYLE TO LUNA X. MILLER,
THE MOON CHILD, WHOSE SENSE OF
FUN INSPIRED GABBY FROM
THE BEGINNING.

FIRST DOSSIER:
WHEN Gabby MET A.L.I.E.N.

WARNING

This book contains revelations so classified that only the most covert layers of the most secretive sects of the Worldwide International Government even know they exist. A single leak could send devastating ripple effects throughout space-time and obliterate the world as we know it.

IF YOU DO NOT BELIEVE YOU CAN HANDLE THE RESPONSIBILITY, WE CANNOT STRESS THIS STRONGLY ENOUGH:

DO NOT TURN THE PAGE.

WELCOME, TRUSTED FRIEND,
TO THE FIRST DOSSIER OF
ASSOCIATE 4118-25125A,
A.K.A. GABBY DURAN,
SITTER TO THE UNSITTABLES.

chapter
ONE

the day that changed Gabby's life started out just like any other ... with a small pitcher of water poured on her head.

"Okay, okay, I'm up!" Gabby spluttered as she bolted upright, though there wasn't anyone to splutter *to*. Gabby was alone. The offending water pitcher had been rigged by her best friend, Zee. It was Zee's solution to Gabby's request for help waking up in the mornings. Zee's first idea was to use her robotics skills to rig Gabby's bed, so at the sound of the alarm it would spring up and catapult Gabby directly onto a beanbag chair across the room. It sounded great . . . until they used a mannequin-Gabby to try Zee's prototype.

The mannequin smashed a giant, Gabby-shaped dent in the back wall.

Zee was sure she could make adjustments and fix the issue, but Gabby opted for Zee's alternate idea instead: the water pitcher. Whenever Gabby pressed the snooze button a third time in a row—*splash!*

It drove Zee apoplectic that after several months of this, Gabby still hit the snooze button that third time. Pavlov's Law demanded that Gabby change her behavior and get out of bed after button-push number two.

Gabby had no answer for this, except to say her love of sleep apparently outweighed the laws of science.

Once she was awake, though, she was unstoppable. She threw off her sopping covers, bundled them up with her equally drenched nightshirt, then stretched her legs over her wild mess of a floor to find the few spots of bare carpet between her bed and her closet. There she dropped her covers long enough to rummage through the tangle of hangers and clothes layering the floor until she found her most comfortable weekend jeans and T-shirt, got dressed, slung her ever-present purple knapsack over her left shoulder, hoisted the giant crumple of bedclothes back into her arms, and picked out a path to her door.

Gabby galloped down her town house's two flights of stairs, deposited her bundle in the dryer and turned it on, then trotted back up to the kitchen, where her mom was juggling a million different pots and pans, all bubbling and steaming and sizzling and giving off such a wild array of smells that Gabby couldn't begin to name a single one.

Okay, her mom wasn't *actually* juggling a million different pots and pans. While the million different pots and pans did their bubbling/steaming/sizzling thing, Alice Duran was *actually* juggling three tomatoes, a feat which she apparently thought would impress Gabby's little sister, Carmen.

"Look, Car! I'm doing it! See? Oh, hi, Gabby!"

The second Alice looked up to say hi to her oldest daughter, all three tomatoes fell unceremoniously to the floor.

Splat! Splat! Splat!

Without looking up from the old-fashioned accounting book on the kitchen table, Carmen said, "Three organic heirloom tomatoes weighing one point five pounds, priced at three dollars and ninety-nine cents per pound, equals 5.985 dollars in the trash."

"Relax, Car," said Gabby. "I think we can eat the six dollars."

"Actually, we can't," Carmen said. "Not anymore. That's the point."

Though only ten, Carmen was as no-nonsense as her

long, flat brown hair with the too-short bangs cut straight across her forehead. "And if you didn't toss your sheets in the dryer every day," she continued to Gabby, "we'd save two hundred sixty-one dollars' worth of electricity."

"Yes, but you'd *lose* two hundred sixty-one dollars' worth of the joy you take in torturing me about it."

"Enough," Alice said as she wrapped her hand in several layers of paper towels ("One quarter Kirkland paper towel roll, at ninety-eight cents a roll, 24.5 cents in the trash," Carmen noted), sopped up the tomato goo, then held it away from her body, so she could pull Gabby into a strong, one-armed embrace.

"Good morning, baby," she said. She gave Gabby a huge kiss right on top of her head, then perked up like a prairie dog. "Do you hear that?" she asked. "It's my baklava calling."

She retreated to her baking corner, which was piled high with a giant stack of phyllo dough. With her Einstein-wild hair and her face and apron smeared with a myriad of splattered colors and textures, Alice looked like a mad scientist as she huddled among her gurgling pots and pans, painting filling onto her pastry. She actually *was* a scientist, or had been before she took up cooking. She'd been a chemist, cooking up concoctions meant to cure the world of all kinds of diseases. But when Gabby and Carmen's dad, an army major, was declared missing in action and presumed dead while Alice was pregnant with Carmen, Alice knew she had to find a way to make money while keeping stay-at-home-mom-ish hours. In no time, cooking cures turned to cooking meals for her catering business, It's All Relativity, a name that played off her look.

Gabby peered into every pot on the stove. She twirled the contents around and inhaled deeply. "Marinara sauce . . . tikka masala . . . and peanut brittle?"

"Pralines," Alice said. "At least they will be. Big Sunday brunch today—a Greek-Italian-Cajun themed Diwali."

Gabby mulled over all the options, then dug into the pantry and grabbed a Pop-Tart, which she slid into the toaster.

"Nutritional content of your choice: zero," Carmen noted.

"You used to worship me, you know," Gabby retorted. "I have video proof."

"It's true," Alice agreed. "When I brought you home from the hospital, only Gabby could make you stop crying."

"It was a psychological experiment," Carmen deadpanned. "I thought you'd be nicer to me if I made you feel important."

"It worked too well," Gabby said. "I feel *so* important that I believe I'm impervious to the evils of Pop-Tartery." She pulled her beautifully browned processed yumminess from the toaster and bounced it between her hands until it cooled enough to hold. "Now what's the scoop?"

"It's what Mom uses to measure out the coffee," Carmen replied as she went back to scribbling in her accounting book.

Gabby never quite knew if Carmen was being exceptionally literal just to mess with her, or because that was how she saw the world. Probably a little of each.

"Got it," Gabby said. "Thanks. And um . . . what's my schedule today?"

Carmen pushed aside the large volume in which she kept track of the family's finances, and replaced it with one of two black binders stacked on the table next to her. The binders looked identical, but Carmen knew one from the other at a glance. One held their mom's schedule, press clippings, and testimonials; the other housed the same information for Gabby.

"Sunday, October eighteenth. Ali, Lia, and Ila. Triplets, age five. Limo to pick you up at—"

A horn sounded from outside the house. Carmen looked at her watch and nodded, pleased by the punctuality.

"—eight A.M. sharp," she finished. "You'll be in the air on the private jet by nine, on set in Florida by eleven, and back home by seven P.M."

"In time to practice my French horn for Friday afternoon's concert!" Gabby said, springing up and heading to the door.

"Where you'll play solo!" Alice cheered.

"Or not," Carmen said. "Maestro Jenkins won't tell her until"—she flipped forward a few pages in the binder dedicated to Gabby—"approximately three fifty-five Friday afternoon."

"Thanks for the vote of confidence, Car," Gabby said.

"It has nothing to do with confidence," Carmen retorted. "Maestro Jenkins never says who will get the solo until five minutes before curtain. Right now it could just as easily be Madison's."

"How do I get you to go back to that wanting-to-make-me-feel-important thing?"

"Can't," Carmen said. "Psychological experiment, re-member?" The tiniest hint of a smirk played at the left corner of her mouth.

"Maestro Jenkins will choose *you*," Alice told Gabby. "I have complete confidence. Got your phone and portable charger?"

"Always."

"Text every hour. If you're in the air and can't, then when you land. Love you!"

"Love you, too!"

Gabby darted out the door and ran down to the curb, where a long black limousine sat waiting. From across the street, she saw Madison Murray framed in her living room's picture window. Madison's perfect blond hair danced gently around her beautiful face as she practiced her flute.

Gabby grimaced. Madison was her archenemy, at least in orchestra. They were both in sixth grade, but they'd played with the Brensville Middle School Orchestra since elementary school. That's how good they were. And while they played very different instruments, they were always up for the same solos. Orchestra leader Maestro Jenkins thought fierce competition was good for his two stars. He tweaked each solo piece just a bit for each instrument, had both Gabby and Madison learn and practice it, then awarded the prize only at the last minute.

Gabby wanted Friday's solo badly, and she'd have a much better shot at it if she were practicing right now, just like Madison. But duty called. Ali, Lia, and Ila needed her, and she couldn't say no to them. Besides, there was still plenty of practice time before the concert.

In her living room, Madison finished a passage and looked up, catching Gabby's eye. Gabby smiled and waved. Madison merely glanced from Gabby to the limousine and back again, then walked pointedly to the window and drew her blinds shut.

It was frustrating. They might be bitter rivals in orchestra, but Gabby always thought that away from the stage, she and Madison should be friends. After all, they had a lot in common. They were both amazing musicians, they'd lived across the street from one another since birth, which was already twelve years now, and . . .

Okay, maybe that was all they had in common. But still, that should be enough! Madison didn't agree, and even though Gabby knew her best friend Zee would say *If someone doesn't have time for you, you shouldn't have time for them*, Gabby still really wanted to win Madison over. She knew she could, too. She just needed the right in.

The limo beeped. Gabby jumped and yanked open the door. She was about to slip inside when something strange caught her eye. A tall, severe-looking older woman stood on the corner. She was dressed all in black and seemed to be staring right at Gabby.

Most of the people in Gabby's neighborhood had lived there for years. Everyone knew everyone else, and the place was a solid car ride from any shopping. This woman was a stranger to Gabby, and strangers didn't generally just find their way here.

Gabby shook off a nervous chill. Most likely the woman was someone's grandmother, here for a visit. Maybe for a funeral, given the outfit.

"Hi!" Gabby called with a smile and wave, but the woman didn't respond. Of course she didn't. She was probably too deep in mourning. Gabby felt awful for disturbing her at a time like this and promised herself she'd ask around the neighborhood when she got back home to find out who had passed away. Then she, Carmen, and Alice could send flowers to the family.

Gabby climbed into the limo and slammed the door shut behind her. "Hi, Albert!" she called.

"Hiya, Gabby," Albert called. "Good to see ya!"

"You, too!"

Gabby settled back to enjoy the ride, but something nagged at her as Albert pulled away from the curb. She turned around in her seat and looked out the back windshield.

The woman in black was still there. And despite the windshield's dark tint, Gabby could swear the woman's eyes were locked directly on to her own.

chapter
TWO

a few hours later, Gabby was sitting in the back of another limo, somewhere in the middle of Florida. The car pulled up to a soundstage, and a tank of a man strode with purpose toward Gabby's door. The man wore tattered army-green pants, with nothing over his ripped-with-muscles chest and abs but two bandoliers of ammunition. A deep scar ran down the left side of his face, the remnant of some long-ago brutality. It twisted his expression into a permanent wicked sneer. With unbelievable force, this man tore open the limousine door, yanked Gabby out by her arm . . .

. . . and pulled her into a huge bear hug.

"Gabby!" he cried. "It's so great to see you!"

Gabby knew that pretty much every other sixth grade girl at Brensville Middle School would die to be in this man's arms right now, but she just didn't think of Adam that way.

"You're doing a *Decimator Four*?" she asked after they pulled out of their hug. She gestured to the telltale scar, but Adam only winked and put a finger to his lips.

"The code title is *Samba Serenade*. Super top secret."

He offered a hand, pinky extended, and Gabby looped her smallest finger through his, swearing to keep mum.

"Is Sierra here, too?" Gabby asked. Sierra Bonita was Adam Dent's wife. The two met when she did the bit part on the first *Decimator* that launched her career, but now she was as big a movie star as him. Maybe even bigger.

"Nah, she's off in Siberia shooting something meaningful," Adam said. "Twenty degrees below zero. Give me action in the heat and humidity any day, am I right?"

"And geckos," Gabby added. She wiggled side to side and climbed her palms through the air, imitating the cute little lizards that always came out at night here, but Adam winced away and shuddered from his chiseled jaw down to his banister-size calves.

"Geckos freak me out," he admitted. "Come on—let's go see the girls. They've missed you like crazy."

"I've missed them, too!" Gabby gushed.

Adam nodded to the security guard at the soundstage door. Like a secret service agent, the guard stood upright and kept his eyes on the field as he held the door open. He didn't even glance at Gabby or Adam. Gabby tried to catch his gaze and give him a friendly hello anyway, but what she saw reflected in his glasses made her voice dry up in her throat.

She wheeled around, her heart racing.

"You okay, Gabby?" Adam asked.

Gabby looked up and down the street. Nothing unusual at all. A couple other soundstages, some golf carts, a few other cars, scattered people walking together to go over business or their lines. . . .

No sign of the tall, severe-looking older woman dressed all in black. The same one she'd seen watching her as she got into the limousine back home. The one she'd seen in the security guard's glasses staring sternly at her from right across the street.

Gabby didn't realize she'd been holding her breath until it came rushing out of her in a long sigh. "I'm fine." She laughed. "Just . . . thought I saw something weird."

"It's a movie lot," Adam said. "There's a lot of something weirds. This morning I had to push past three zombies and an elephant just to get coffee. Come on."

Gabby followed him into the soundstage, glancing back into the guard's glasses on the way in. This time she saw nothing unusual, but why would she? There was no way the old woman could possibly be here.

It must be the humidity. It was messing with her mind. Good thing the stage was air-conditioned. The rush of cold air woke her up inside, and all other thoughts disappeared as she marveled at the incredible giant-size scenery. This *Decimator* apparently took place in New York City, after some near-cataclysmic event for the Earth. Wreckage of buildings lay in massive, crazy-shaped piles. Even the Statue of Liberty was there. Or at least her head. It was sandwiched between a fallen radio tower and half a billboard for a Broadway show.

Two five-year-old girls crawled over it like ants.

"Wheeee!" one of them cried as she slid down a prong of the statue's crown.

"No!" screamed a man in jeans and a T-shirt. The way everyone on set watched him, Gabby assumed he must be the director. "You have to get off!"

The probably director growled to a young man standing next to him holding a clipboard. "This is insane. I swear, if Adam Dent wasn't the biggest movie star in the world right now . . ."

"Look at me!" cried the other little girl. She stood next to Lady Liberty, pushed one finger into the giant plaster left nostril, and twisted it back and forth.

"NO!" wailed the director. "That's the Statue of Liberty!

You can't pick her nose!"

"To be fair," Adam interjected as he and Gabby drew close, "we *did* decapitate her."

The director wheeled around and his entire demeanor changed. "Adam!" He beamed. "Yes! Excellent point. Adorable girls. But, um . . . isn't your assistant supposed to be watching them?"

"She was, yeah," Adam said, then called out, "Romina?"

"She's right here, Daddy! Look! I did it all by myself!"

This was a third little girl, and Adam followed her voice to another corner of the soundstage. The girl stood triumphantly next to a frazzled-looking dark-haired young woman who wore glasses, a gag around her mouth, and handcuffs on her wrists and ankles. Adam smiled.

"Hey, that's great technique! You remembered that from my last film!" Adam knelt down to get face-to-face with his handcuffed assistant. "So you and the girls are having fun?"

Romina responded with a series of gag-bound *mmmph*s.

"Oh right!" Adam realized. He loosened the gag, leaving Romina free to gasp for breath.

"Great fun," she said semi-convincingly. Then she noticed Gabby and her eyes went wide. "Gabby! I'm so glad you're here!"

The second they heard her name, all three little girls wheeled around, their eyes aglow.

"GABBY!" they screamed in unison. They ran and leaped on top of her, tackling her to the ground as each one scrambled for the first hug. Gabby laughed and did her best to wrap her arms around all three of them at once.

"Okay, you have to let me get up," Gabby said. "I need to look at you! Two candy bars each if I can't tell you apart!"

Like cadets falling in line, the five-year-olds sprung off Gabby and stood at attention.

"Um, Gabby," Adam began, "I don't know about the candy bar thing. Sierra keeps them gluten/dairy/sugar-free."

"It's okay," Gabby assured him as she walked up and down the row of triplets. "They won't win."

"But Gabby . . . *I* can't even tell them apart."

Adam had reason to be nervous. The three girls stood exactly the same height, and each wore identical denim shorts with the exact same green-and-white striped shirts and identical black canvas sneakers. While they each wore mismatched socks, they wore the *same* mismatched socks: purple anklets with blue stars on the left foot, red knee-highs with pink polka dots on the right. Their blond hair was fashioned in the same asymmetrical bobs, with bangs the exact same length falling over their right eyes.

They even had matching scabs on their knees.

Gabby knew she was at a disadvantage, but she wasn't worried. She clasped her hands behind her back, plastered on her best knowing-detective look, and paced in front of the girls. As she reached each one she spun toward her, raising one brow and leaning in close to fix the triplet in question with a piercing stare.

The girl in the center giggled. Just the littlest bit, but it was enough.

"Ila!" Gabby shouted, pointing to her.

Ila always broke first.

"How did you know?!" the little girl squealed.

"My freckles give me psychic powers," Gabby intoned. "Now, don't tell me . . ."

Gabby got down on her knees and swayed back and forth, looking from one end-triplet to the other. Ali and Lia were good; they stood identically stone-faced. Luckily, Gabby wasn't looking at their faces. She glanced down and saw the triplet on the far right gently drumming her fingers against her leg, just like Lia always did when she forced herself to be still.

"My freckles are revealing the answer . . ." Gabby said, dramatically closing her eyes and placing her fingers to her temples. "You're . . . Lia!"

"Yes!" Lia cheered.

Adam shook his head, amazed. "Pretty terrific, Gabby."

"Gabby's the best!" Lia agreed.

"No fair!" Ali sulked. "I wanted the candy bar."

"Oh, I have something way better than candy bars," Gabby assured the girls. "My psychic freckles are telling me the perfect game. Want to hear it?"

The girls did. They leaned into her like daisies reaching for the sun. But before Gabby could speak, Romina cleared her throat.

"I'm sorry," the handcuffed assistant interrupted, "but can you get me out of these?"

"Oh right," Adam said, then turned to his daughters. "Which one of you has the key?"

"I do," Ali said brightly . . . but then her face fell in an impishly exaggerated frown as she rubbed her stomach. "In my belly."

"In your *what*?!" Romina wailed.

"Actually, it *was* in my belly," Ali amended, "until . . ."

She mimed flushing a toilet, making the whooshing and gurgling sounds with her mouth. Romina's jaw dropped.

"Oooh," Adam clucked. "That's a toughie. Maybe we should call special effects? They blow up buildings; I bet they can blow off the handcuffs."

"*Blow* off?!" Romina cried.

Gabby bent down and whispered to the girls. "This is gonna take a while. How 'bout we go play?"

The triplets nodded eagerly and, like little ducklings, followed Gabby to the back of the soundstage. Everyone around stopped and stared. It was the first time since the shoot started that the tiny trio wasn't wreaking havoc on the set.

"It'll never last," the director muttered to his assistant. "Within the hour they'll be back ruining the shoot, or I'll give you my sports car."

Much to the delight of the assistant, who drove away that night in a shiny red convertible, Gabby had a plan. She waited until she and the girls were out of earshot of anyone else, then crouched down low and beckoned them close, all the while glancing around as if to make sure no one was listening in.

The girls were curious—what was Gabby trying to hide? They huddled nearer to her.

"I'm actually here on a mission," Gabby admitted, pushing a lock of brown curls behind her ear, "and I need the three of you to help."

"A spy mission?" Ila asked.

Gabby nodded. "A *secret* spy mission. But it'll only work if we stay *supremely* quiet, and don't let anyone see us for even a second."

The triplets nodded. This was obviously very important.

"Somewhere in these halls"—she gestured behind her, away from the set, to the hallways dotted with dressing rooms, catering stations, working carpenters, prop collections, and wardrobe areas—"is a wooden turtle. Not just any turtle—a secret spy turtle filled with secret spy codes. Our mission is to find it."

The girls were entranced. They hung on Gabby's every word as she pulled from her purple knapsack the tools of their spy trade: little notebooks and pens they'd use to draw pictures and make notes about everything they saw. She gave them the plan: they'd go into each room together, quiet as mice, then spread out and scope the scene without touching a thing or letting anyone know they were there. They'd communicate with hand signals, which Gabby took time to teach them well. After each new room they'd huddle together and whisper about what they found, discuss their upcoming plan of action for turtle hunting in the next room, then continue on with the search.

For thirty minutes the triplets sat rapt. Then they started their mission.

It went flawlessly.

For the rest of the afternoon, the girls and Gabby were as invisible as whispers. Pointedly avoiding any area where they might interfere with the movie shoot, Gabby led the team of super-spies through every room. They made no sounds and disturbed nothing. They took copious notes in their notebooks and exchanged intricate hand signals conveying their many suspicions about everyone they saw. Sure, the crew members looked harmless, but on closer inspection they were clearly secret-spy-turtle-thieves mired in deception and conspiracy. Not even their dad was beyond suspicion.

Gabby waited until the shooting day was almost over, then pulled the girls together to share their clues in hushed whispers.

"What do you think?" she asked, pulling out her own pencil and notebook to compile their thoughts. "Any idea where the turtle is?"

"I know! I know!" Ila jumped up and down and waved her arm in the air. "It was stolen by the woman in black!"

"One of the stagehands," Gabby scribbled, nodding knowingly. "I wonder what plans she has for the turtle's secret codes."

"Not one of the stagehands!" Ila said. "I mean the *old* woman in black!"

Gabby's pencil froze. "The *old* woman in black?"

"Uh-huh," Ali agreed. "I saw her, too. She was *really* old. And she stood super-tall, like she was being stretched up to the sky."

Gabby remembered the old woman who stared at her back in her neighborhood. *She* stood tall like that, too.

And so did a million wicked stepmothers in kids' movies, Gabby reminded herself. Plus, the triplets were little—their idea of "really old" probably wasn't the same as her own.

Gabby forced herself to put silly ideas out of her head

and keep writing. "Okay," she said, "this is good stuff. What else can you tell me about the old woman in black?"

"She was like magic," Lia whispered. "She'd be in a room and I'd see her out of the corner of my eye, but when I looked right at her . . . *poof!*"

"She disappeared? Like in a puff of smoke?" Gabby asked the question hopefully. If the woman poofed in and out of existence, she was definitely a figment of the girls' imaginations.

"No!" Lia retorted. "She wasn't magic, she had *skills*."

"Ninja skills!" Ila added, and demonstrated with a whirling air kick that landed her flat on her bottom. It didn't faze her. She rolled to her knees and pointed a tiny finger in Gabby's face. "And she knew *you* were our leader. Every time I saw her, she was staring right at you."

"Like she was tracking your every move!" Ali added eagerly.

"And wouldn't rest until she'd followed you to the ends of the earth!" Lia finished.

Gabby clutched her pencil so tightly it snapped in her grip. "Ow!" she yelped as a splinter sliced into her finger.

"Gabby!"

"Are you okay?"

"Can we help?"

The three girls huddled around Gabby, concerned. While they examined her shaking hand, Gabby nervously scanned the room, half-expecting the old woman in black to leap out of the shadows and attack her.

No one was there. No one unexpected, at least. Just the regular crowd of people working on the movie; all of them too busy to pay attention to Gabby and the girls.

Gabby took a deep breath. It had to be a coincidence. Even if the girls *had* seen a black-clad old woman around the soundstage, that didn't mean it was the same woman Gabby had seen at home. The woman could still be a stagehand. Or she could be the person Gabby thought she saw reflected in the security guard's glasses. Gabby had jumped to the conclusion that the reflection was the woman from her neighborhood, but it made far more sense that she was actually an extra, or a caterer, or even an Adam Dent fan who snuck her way onto the set. That wouldn't explain her following Gabby around and staring at her, but that part could easily be the girls' imagination.

Gabby concentrated on doctoring her splinter. She let the girls help, and by the time they were done and the stage manager called a wrap, Gabby felt much more relaxed. She made a show of studying the clues the girls had gathered all day and determined that according to their calculations, the turtle with the secret spy codes should be in a prop cannon— the same prop cannon in which Gabby had secretly hidden it earlier in the day. The triplets' screams of delight when they found it brought their dad running.

"Hey!" he exclaimed. "There you are! Is everything okay? You guys were so quiet all day I got worried!"

"We found the turtle!" Ila cried.

"The old ninja woman wanted it, but we thwarted her!" Ali added.

Lia held the turtle high in triumph. "Now we can save the planet from Ninja-Nana Annihilation!"

As the girls jumped and cheered, Adam scrunched his face in thought. "Ninja-Nana Annihilation?" He paused a second, then shouted out to the director, "Reggie! Come here! I think we need to do some rewrites!" Then he wrapped Gabby in a huge hug. "Thanks a million for today, Gabby. You're a lifesaver. You'll do it again?"

"I don't know . . ." Gabby sucked on her teeth like it was a tough call. "Only if the girls *really* want—"

"YES!!!" they chorused, hurling themselves on her for a giant group hug that they only gave up when Gabby threatened to use her psychic freckles to find their ultimate tickle spots. As the girls squealed and ran off, Romina came over to escort Gabby back to the waiting limo.

As the car sped away, Gabby sprawled back in the seat. She giggled, imaging a *Decimator Four* filled with evil old women doing backflips while chasing secret wooden turtles. She'd have to take her friend Satchel to see it in 3-D. The two of them loved cheesy movies, the splatterier the better. They'd been watching them together since birth. Or more precisely, since a week after their same-day births, when their maternity-ward-roomie moms had gotten together to share labor videos. Ugh.

The limo took Gabby to the Bonita-Dents' private jet, where Gabby spent the flight feasting on steak and thick-cut fries. The meal was so giant, Gabby insisted Amelia, the flight attendant, share it with her, and the two chatted happily for most of the flight. When Amelia had to prepare for landing, Gabby leaned back and hummed the solo for Friday afternoon's concert while she pantomimed the finger motions on an imaginary French horn. It wouldn't be as effective as Madison's practice session, but it was something. She got so lost in the notes that she went from the airplane to the limo waiting to take her home in a musical daze. Only when she finished humming the solo did she look up to smile apologetically to the driver.

"Hi, Alber—" she started.

But her voice stuck in her throat when she realized the cold, dark eyes staring at her in the rearview mirror weren't Albert's at all.

Someone else was driving the car.

An old woman, dressed in black.

And the woman did *not* look pleased.

chapter
THREE

*g*abby lunged for the door and tried to throw it open, but the lock clicked shut.

"I wouldn't do that," the woman's icy voice said. "Unwise to leap from a moving car. And you struck me as so intelligent."

The woman was right. Jumping from the car would be highly hazardous to Gabby's health and her chances of getting Friday's solo, which would be impossible to play from a hospital bed. Still, Gabby couldn't peel her hands off the door handle. She was frozen in place. Only her eyes moved, to stare back at the face in the rearview mirror.

It wasn't a coincidence this time. It couldn't be. That face was the same one she saw reflected in the security guard's glasses in Florida. The same one she saw in her own neighborhood that morning.

But how? And why?

Gabby took a deep breath and tried to slow her thundering heart. She was stuck in this car now, at the mercy of this stalker, and she'd be much better equipped to escape if she stayed calm. She forced a laugh and said, "Sorry about that. I guess you startled me. I thought you'd be someone else."

"Intriguing," the woman said with a nod. "Because so far, Gabby Duran, *you* are *exactly* who I'd hoped you'd be. Aside from the near lemminglike leap to oblivion, of course. That I must admit was disappointing."

Gabby was stunned. "You know my name."

"I know many things."

Outside the window, Gabby watched her exit whiz by. "Um . . . I think we need to turn around," Gabby said. "I live that way."

As she spoke, she eased open her purple knapsack. If she moved slowly and didn't get the woman's attention, she could sneak out her phone and dial 911.

"You can call the authorities if you'd like," the woman said. "But I have no intention of harming you. Quite the opposite. I have a proposition for you. One I believe you'll find intriguing, and one you won't get to hear should you report this event to another human being. Or electronic device, in case you imagined that was a loophole."

Gabby *had* thought that was a loophole. If she texted her mom, she wouldn't *technically* be reporting directly to another human being. So much for that idea.

"You were in front of my house this morning," Gabby said. "And at the studio in Florida."

"And cats bathe by licking themselves, and Henry the Eighth had six wives," the woman sighed. "Would you like to recite more facts I already know?"

Gabby felt chastened, even though she was fairly sure she was the one being wronged in this situation. She sat a little straighter and challenged the woman. "What if I don't want to hear your proposition? What if I tell you to immediately turn this car around and take me home?"

"Well, I certainly hope you'd have the decency to ask rather than tell me, but if you indeed made such a request, I would do just that. After admonishing you for carelessly splitting infinitives, of course. But then you'd never know what you'd missed."

Gabby leaned back in her seat, considering. She wasn't afraid anymore. She supposed she should be. An interstate stalker who spoke in cryptic promises and drove Gabby away from home without asking first was pretty much a textbook call-for-help situation. Yet the more she spoke with the old woman, the less frightened she became. The woman's voice had the clipped tones of a no-nonsense boarding school headmistress. It was the kind of voice that didn't suffer fools and wouldn't waste time on lies. If she said she wouldn't harm Gabby and would take her home if she asked, Gabby believed her.

"Well?" the woman asked. "Would you like to hear my offer?"

Gabby imagined telling the story of this moment to the people she loved most. Carmen would accuse her of idiocy and Alice would worry about her safety. Both would want her to turn around and go home. Satchel would vote for home, too. Much as he could handle anything on a movie screen, in real life he'd freak out if he stepped on a crack or spilled salt. This would have him hyperventilating.

Then she heard Zee's voice in her head. *It's always better to know than not know. Always.*

Gabby smiled. Those were the words Zee said when they'd bonded as lab partners in fourth grade and wondered how much Jell-O powder it would take to turn the school pool into a gelatinous dessert. Gabby had agreed then, and she agreed just as much now. Besides, hearing what the woman had to say didn't commit her to anything.

Still, she felt she had a right to make a demand—a

request—of her own. "First, I'd like to know your name," she said.

"You may call me Edwina," the woman replied.

"Because that's your name?"

"Because it will suffice."

Gabby still didn't say yes. She took a moment to study Edwina. The triplets had thought she was ancient. She wasn't quite that, but the deep lines along her forehead and down her cheeks did peg her as older, maybe even seventy. The white hair piled into a tight bun beneath her chauffeur's cap also aged her. Only her brown eyes seemed young and strong. They were sharp and piercing, filled with keen intelligence. Gabby understood why the triplets had found the woman intimidating, but she highly doubted Edwina had ninja skills. She imagined her leaping into a midair roundhouse kick and laughed out loud.

Edwina raised an eyebrow. "You don't think I could pull off Ninja-Nana Annihilation?"

Gabby clamped her hand over her mouth, then asked, "How did you . . . ?"

"No, I don't read minds," Edwina said, "not even to know you were wondering if I did. I simply surmised it from a combination of your clumsy attempt to subtly size me up, your expression, and what I observed earlier."

Gabby opened her mouth to reply, but she was too

shocked for anything to come out. A hint of a smile played on Edwina's lips.

"Magnificent work, by the way," Edwina said. "With the triplets. You handled them beautifully."

"I didn't *handle* them," Gabby corrected her immediately. "I played with them. It was fun. They're really good kids."

"For *you*," Edwina noted. "As are many children who are impossible for other authority figures."

Gabby screwed up her face. "I'm not an 'authority figure.' I'm just a babysitter."

"*Just* a babysitter?" Edwina arched an eyebrow. "That's not what I've heard. More like a *super*-sitter. Clients all over the world seek you out for the most impossible babysitting cases."

Gabby simply nodded. She was proud of her reputation and happy she could help people who needed her, but she didn't like to brag about it. Starting with her own little sister—despite Carmen's claims otherwise—babysitting was just something Gabby was good at. It came naturally to her.

"Tell me," Edwina said, narrowing her eyes. "What's your secret?"

"I don't have one," Gabby said honestly. "I just love kids."

"*All* kids?" Edwina pressed.

"Never met one I didn't like."

"No matter how . . . unusual?"

Gabby laughed. "The more unusual the better! That's what makes babysitting so fun. Every kid is unique and different, so I never do the same thing twice."

Edwina nodded thoughtfully, then stared at the road and didn't say anything for what felt like ages. Gabby wondered if she'd put her foot in her mouth again, and if Edwina wouldn't offer the proposition after all. She was running their entire conversation back through her head when Edwina's eyes snapped to the rearview mirror and caught Gabby's own.

"I have a job for you," Edwina offered. "One boy, eight years old, ten minutes. I'll pay you four times your hourly rate."

Gabby sat straight up and leaned forward against the seat belt. "What?!"

"I believe you heard me," Edwina said. "Should this job go well, I'll offer you more."

The "Yes!" was about to leap from Gabby's mouth, but Edwina cut her off.

"Before you answer, there's a caveat. You must agree beforehand that you will tell no one about the experience. Not your mother, not your sister, not your friends."

Gabby fell back into her seat. This changed things. "I don't like to lie," she said.

"Nor do I," said Edwina. "It's an admirable quality. However, I'm afraid the circumstance requires it. So what do you say? Are the terms acceptable to you?"

A million conflicting thoughts whirled through Gabby's brain, but only one got bigger and bigger until it stood front and center in her mind.

Gabby's mom, Alice.

She worked so hard to provide for Gabby and Carmen and still be there with the girls all the time, but it was a struggle. Though Alice never complained about it, Gabby knew her mom always felt the pressure to earn more money in less time. And yes, Gabby's income helped, but between school and her French horn and homework and time with her friends, she could only work so many hours. If Edwina really would pay four times her rate, that could make a huge difference in the Durans' lives.

There was something else Gabby wanted, too, but she knew she shouldn't get ahead of herself. Right now Edwina was offering just the one ten-minute job. A nice bonus. A little extra she could put aside and use for something special.

Gabby checked her watch, then picked up her phone.

"Your hourly check-in text to your mother?" Edwina asked.

Gabby wasn't even surprised anymore by how much Edwina knew. She simply nodded, typed, *All good, but running about an hour late b/c of plane stuff. Love u!*, and pressed Send. She felt a twinge of guilt, but it faded. She was doing a little wrong for a greater right. Or at least the opportunity for a greater right. She looked into the rearview mirror and met Edwina's eyes.

"I accept your offer."

Edwina nodded almost imperceptibly and remained silent for the rest of the ride.

Five minutes later, they pulled onto a tree-lined lane with wide sidewalks and houses with lovingly manicured yards. It was early evening, but a dozen different kids still raced around on foot, bikes, or skates. The charming cookie-cutter homes were all spread far enough apart to offer privacy but close enough that neighbors would grow naturally friendly.

The road ended in the swell of a cul-de-sac. Edwina pulled up in front of a green house with white shutters, where a gray Persian fuzzball of a cat rose languidly in the window, stretched, then hopped out of sight.

"Aw!" Gabby cooed. "They have a kitten!"

"Of sorts," Edwina replied.

Gabby understood. The cat had looked small but was probably full-grown. Still, it was really cute. Maybe she and the eight-year-old would find a string and play with it for ten minutes. Easiest assignment ever!

Still playing proper limo driver, Edwina exited the car, then came around to open the door for Gabby. The two walked through the gate in the white picket fence surrounding the front yard, then up a flagstone path to the door.

Edwina made no move to knock or ring the bell. She didn't have to. The second they neared the house, the door swung open to reveal a smiling young couple so beautiful, fresh-faced, and happy they might have stepped off the pages of *Perfect Parent* magazine. They even held hands just to answer the door. Gabby liked them immediately.

"You must be Gabby!" they said in unison.

Exact unison. Even their inflections matched. It was the vocal equivalent of being with Ali, Lia, and Ila all over again.

Odd, but sweet.

"I am. Gabby Duran. Nice to meet you."

"No, it's nice to meet *you*," the smiling dad said.

"Please come in!" the smiling mom offered.

"Can we get you anything?" the dad asked. "Water? Coffee?"

The mom's smile strained a bit, and Gabby noticed her squeeze his hand a little harder. "John, honey," she said tightly, "Gabby's still a little girl. Little girls don't drink coffee. All humans know that."

"Of course!" John laughed, but it sounded a little forced. "I was just kidding. So was my wife, Lisa, when she said 'all humans.' I mean, who talks like that?"

Lisa stiffened as if she'd realized she'd made a horrible mistake, but the moment passed so quickly Gabby almost thought she'd imagined it, and a heartbeat later Lisa was laughing right along with her husband.

Loudly. And for a strangely long time.

Edwina sighed and rolled her eyes. "May we see the boy?"

"Of course!" John and Lisa chorused. They turned around but didn't release each other's hands. So instead of simply pivoting, they walked awkwardly around each other in a large circle while Edwina sighed and tapped a foot impatiently.

"This is ridiculous," Edwina finally snapped. "Gabby, come with me."

She walked briskly down the hall and opened a door, revealing stairs leading to a basement. The stairs turned before they made it all the way down, so Gabby couldn't see much of the room from where she stood. Still, she could tell it was finished, with sky-blue painted walls and a thick sandy-brown carpet. Music wafted up, and Gabby heard the jangling of a bell—maybe the cat? Gabby hadn't seen it since she came inside, so maybe John and Lisa had let it downstairs. She also heard boyish laughter.

"Your charge is down there," Edwina said, nodding down the stairs. "I'll fetch you in ten minutes."

"Got it," Gabby said.

She stepped onto the staircase, and the door instantly slammed behind her.

Click.

Had Edwina locked her in?

For the first time, Gabby felt a prickle of unease and

wondered if she'd made a big mistake coming here.

"Hey, did you hear that?" she heard the boy ask. "Is that my babysitter?"

Feet pounded across the floor and onto the stairs, and a moment later a towheaded mop top appeared on the landing just below Gabby. He was small for eight, but everything else was exactly what Gabby would expect from a kid with lots of energy. The shins of his jeans looked like they'd lost a brutal battle with a grassy field, his T-shirt had a juice stain down the front, and his hair stuck up wildly on one side. The cat had followed him, and now looked up at him curiously, as if wondering when they'd get back to whatever they were doing. The boy, however, was all about Gabby.

"It *is* you!" he said with a giddy smile. "I'm Philip. Are you here to play with me?"

Gabby laughed at her own misgivings. Philip was a great kid—anyone could see that. Why would Edwina imagine she'd have to pay Gabby four times her hourly rate to spend ten minutes with him?

"I am!" Gabby assured him. "And I'm so excited! What do you want to play?"

"Oh, I know all kinds of games!" Philip enthused. He slipped his little hand in Gabby's and pulled her with him back down the stairs. The basement was all playroom: huge and carpeted, with stacks of toys, scattered beanbag chairs, and lots of empty space to run around.

Gabby shrugged her purple knapsack off her shoulders and knelt down, so she and Philip were eye to eye. "Tell you what," she said. "We don't have a ton of time this playdate, so how about you show me your *favorite* game."

"Okay!" Philip agreed. "I call this one The Brand-New Babysitter and the Giant . . ."

Philip's voice dropped three octaves as he said the word "Giant." His deep rumbling tone filled the room and shook the very walls.

". . . Drippy . . ." the booming voice continued, but now Philip's skin started to bubble and pucker. His clothes seemed to melt *into* his skin, like they weren't fabric at all but part of a body that was now changing . . . and growing by the second.

". . . SLUG-MONSTER!" Philip's deep rumbling voice finished with a shout. He had swelled until he was taller than Gabby herself, and his human body had bubbled and oozed away entirely, leaving a massive curl of gelatinous ooze topped by two googly eyeballs on long stalks. These hung down close in front of Gabby's face, and the creature-formerly-known-as-Philip's mouth opened in a drooling, saber-toothed grin.

"So . . . what do you think of my game?" it asked.

chapter FOUR

*E*dwina sat at the kitchen table, casually thumbing through e-mails on her tablet. None of the sounds wafting up from the basement fazed her. Not the pounding of racing feet, not the wild jiggling of the locked door, not the bloodcurdling screams.

John and Lisa weren't faring quite so well.

"I really wish you wouldn't drink that stuff," Lisa told her husband as she paced the floor. "It's so high-octane."

John lowered the red gasoline container from his mouth and said pointedly, "At least I'm not the one biting my nails."

Lisa removed her hand from the candy dish full of metal fasteners. "They're screws, actually," she said tightly. "And I can't help it. I eat when I'm anxious."

A massive crash from downstairs made both parents jump. Lisa raced to Edwina. "Can't we just open the door and check? Gabby seemed so sweet. I can't live with myself if she ends up like the girl who tried to help the Blitzfarbs."

Edwina didn't answer. She looked up from the tablet and met Lisa's eyes just long enough to communicate that the interruption was most unappreciated. Then she gazed down again. Lisa went back to pacing and chewing on screws. John stopped drinking, but he nervously dangled his eyes in and out of their sockets.

Finally, Edwina's tablet beeped.

"It is time," she said.

"Oh, thank goodness," Lisa gushed. She raced for the basement door and flung it open. The cat was right there. It stood on its back legs and had one of its front paws raised, as if it had been about to knock on the door itself.

"Good, you're here," the cat said in a sweet feminine drawl, "'Cause believe me, y'all don't want to miss this."

Remaining on her back legs, the cat led Lisa, John, and Edwina down the stairs. As they turned the corner, Lisa gasped. The basement was a shambles. The sky-blue walls were riddled with dents, patches of carpet were shredded to bits, and several beanbag chairs had been ferociously gutted, their innards spilled across the floor.

John put a hand on his wife's shoulder. "We're too late," he intoned.

"For the love of Zinqual, will you please keep moving?" Edwina asked sharply. When the parents wouldn't, Edwina sighed and pushed her way past them until she'd fully descended the stairs and could take in the entire room.

"Shhh," Gabby said. "He's napping."

Gabby sat in the one intact beanbag chair. In one hand she held a copy of *Better Homes and Gardens*. With her other she stroked the back of Philip's gelatinous head, which lay in her lap. The rest of his body sprawled across the floor.

"We were playing his favorite game," she whispered to Edwina. "He got really into it—tired him right out, so I read him stories until he fell asleep." She indicated the magazine. "He said he likes this one because it's scary: 'Top Ten Ways to Eradicate Slugs.'" Gabby shuddered. "Gave us the shivers too, right, Vondlejax?"

The cat had made her way to Gabby's side and leaned one elbow on the beanbag chair. "You know it, honeylamb. My tail was so far between my legs I could've tickled my own chin!"

Gabby laughed, then turned to Philip's parents. "I'm so sorry about the furniture. It's my fault. I have to admit I got a little nervous when he first . . . you know."

"A little?" Vondlejax teased. "Sweetcheeks, I thought I'd have to run you to my litter box!"

Gabby let out an embarrassed laugh. "A lot nervous. Pretty completely terrified, to be honest." Then she turned to the cat. "You didn't exactly help."

"I declare, I most certainly did! I shouted right out, 'Don't you panic! Every little thing's gonna be just peaches and cream!'"

Gabby tilted her head and looked at Vondlejax. The cat cleared her throat.

". . . which I suppose might have been a teensy weensy shock," Vondlejax admitted, "seein' as you thought I was an ordinary house cat."

"I *did* panic," Gabby said apologetically to Philip's parents, "and I ran and knocked into some things. . . . I may have even screamed a little. . . ."

"You think?" Vondlejax hooted.

"But then . . ." Lisa stammered, "how did you . . ."

John finished for her. "What changed?"

"Well," Gabby said, "before Philip . . . altered himself, he said he wanted to play a game. So even though I was really scared when he was chasing me, I realized that's what it was to him, a game. But it wasn't a nice game, you know? I mean, he might look like a monster—sorry—but that doesn't mean he is one. He's just a kid. And it's kind of awful that he knows someone like me who's supposed to take care of him is going to run away screaming. It made me really sad."

Lisa sniffled loudly. "That's the nicest thing I've ever heard a human say," she sobbed. John handed her a tissue, and she blotted the tears that trickled from her elbow.

"You ain't heard nothin' yet," Vondlejax said as she leaped onto the back of the couch. "Our girl Gabby spun around all upon a sudden and cried out, 'Now it's my turn to chase you!' Oh, was that boy surprised." The cat fanned herself with a paw and Gabby laughed.

"It's true," she said. "I think that's when we did the most damage down here. But he was having fun. Real fun. I could tell. And then he got sleepy."

Gabby smiled down at Philip. His head was still in her lap. Careful not to wake him, she gave him a gentle hug. Her arm sank a bit into his gooey skin. He sighed happily in his sleep.

John knelt down next to Gabby. "Would you like to move in with us?" he asked. "Forever?"

"Come now, that's hardly appropriate," Edwina clucked. "In fact, it's time for me to get Gabby home. A little assistance, please?"

Lisa gently lifted her son's head so Gabby could slip off the beanbag chair without waking him. Gabby grabbed her purple knapsack, then before she got up she knelt down in front of Vondlejax. The cat used both front paws to scratch behind Gabby's ears. "See?" Vondlejax cooed. "Right there, just like that. Isn't that just pure heaven?"

"You were right," Gabby said. "It feels incredible, thanks."

She gave the cat a hand-to-paw high five, then blew Philip a kiss before she followed Edwina back upstairs and toward the front door. John and Lisa shadowed their every step.

"So when exactly *are* you available?" John asked.

"Do you work during the school week?" Lisa added.

"Do you have room for any more regular clients?"

"How many months ahead can we book?"

Gabby started the same answer she gave all her new clients. "Just call my sister. She—"

"*I* will let you know when and if Gabby's available," Edwina cut her off. "Let us remember, she isn't officially in the program yet."

Before Gabby could say another word, Edwina herded her outside and back into the limousine. Gabby immediately rolled down the window. It was dark outside, but the front porch was well lit, and Gabby could clearly see John, Lisa, and Vondlejax.

"Good-bye!" Gabby called. "It was wonderful meeting you! I hope to see you again soon!"

The threesome all waved back. Then John nudged

Vondlejax, who quickly dropped to all four paws and began an intensive and very feline tongue bath. Gabby kept waving until the house was out of sight, then she rolled up the window. She tried to sit back in her seat, but suddenly she couldn't breathe. She sat straighter, tilting her neck back to gasp for air. Her body trembled all over. Even her stomach felt fluttery.

"There's a thick blanket under the seat," Edwina said. "I recommend wrapping yourself up."

Gabby reached down and felt thick fuzziness. She gratefully pulled the blanket around her and huddled into it. "I don't understand," she chattered. "I'm not scared. Not anymore."

"Delayed shock," Edwina said. "It happens. Much like when you force yourself to be brave for an injection, but faint when you get up to leave. Keep warm. It'll pass."

She turned up the heat in the back of the car.

Gabby felt frighteningly out of control of her own body. She cuddled deeper into the thick blanket and concentrated on the warm air bathing her face. Soon her teeth stopped chattering and her breathing slowed. She was okay. She took a long, deep breath and let it out with a sigh as she relaxed into the seat.

"It was your sister, yes?" Edwina asked.

Gabby's jaw clenched. She was always wary when people

asked about Carmen. "What do you mean?"

"The child who didn't deserve to be treated like a monster," Edwina said. "Seemed like you had a good understanding of what that might be like."

Gabby narrowed her eyes and glared at Edwina through the rearview mirror, but the older woman didn't look critical, just matter-of-fact. Maybe even a little . . . kind? It made Gabby let her guard down.

"Yeah," she admitted. "That was Car. She was tough when she was little. She didn't know how to deal when stuff made her uncomfortable . . . and a lot of stuff made her uncomfortable. So she screamed . . . or yanked at her own hair . . . or threw things. . . . It was no big deal, I knew how to calm her down. But people didn't get it. They stared. Or they didn't stare, but only because they were working really hard *not* to stare, which was worse. Like she was too horrible to even look at. She wasn't. She just needed someone to understand her."

Gabby fiddled with her knapsack. She didn't like to talk about when Carmen was little. It felt disloyal, like she'd just tainted Edwina's vision of her sister.

"All people need someone to understand them," Edwina said. "Just like Philip."

Raising her eyes to look back at Edwina, Gabby said, "But Philip isn't exactly a *person* . . . right?"

"There's something I'd like you to read," Edwina said.

She pressed a button on the front console and the television screen in the limo's backseat sprang to life. On it, a glowing green insignia rotated inside a circle—a logo, it seemed—and next to it glowed the words:

Association
Linking
Intergalactics and
Earthlings as
Neighbors

"A.L.I.E.N.," Gabby read the acronym. "Are you saying Philip's an *alien*? Like . . . from-another-planet alien?"

Edwina pulled her tablet out of her bag and handed it back to Gabby. The screen held scans of several newspaper clippings, each cut off mid-article. "Read," she said.

Gabby read.

From the *Philadelphia News Report*, August 30, 1955:

SINKHOLE SWALLOWS SITTER

Emergency workers were thrilled to report the rescue of Abigail Latrelle, 16, after a most harrowing experience. She was babysitting three young children when a giant sinkhole opened and swallowed her whole.

"We built a fort out back," she said. "The kids wanted to give it a basement, but I said we couldn't dig up their yard. They said they'd handle that part themselves, and the next thing I knew, the kids were glowing bright red and the ground was collapsing under me!"

Clearly, there are some strange elements to Ms. Latrelle's story. While doctors have given her a clean bill of health, they do believe the shock of falling into the sinkhole might contribute to her delusions.

From the *Miami Gazette*, March 5, 1985:

SCARED SIT-LESS!

How young is too young to babysit? Ronnie Jacobson's parents thought thirteen was the perfect age for their son to sit for their young neighbors. Yet if the story he brought home is any indication, the choice may have been premature.

In the middle of his babysitting job, Ronnie abandoned his charges, raced home, and locked himself in his room. The kids, he claimed, had "turned themselves into mice and crawled all over" him, scaring him so badly he refused to go back.

Thankfully, the story has a happy ending in that Ronnie's parents went to their neighbors' house and found the children safe and sound, albeit covered in shreds of finely nibbled cheese. Still the tale stands as caution to parents of aspiring sitters who might not be ready for the responsibility.

From the *San Francisco Journal*, October 30, 2008:

BABYSITTERS GET VAMPIRE FEVER

We all know the Twilight Saga is an international teen obsession, but nowhere has that been more evident than on Sitipedia. The site touts itself as "the free encyclopedia for all things babysitting." Like Wikipedia, anyone can contribute to articles on the site, and no entry has attracted more traffic

than one entitled "Babysitting Vampires."

Apparently, hundreds of thousands of babysitting teens across the world are convinced that the children left in their care are indeed bloodsucking vampires. To share their experiences and offer advice to others, they constantly expand the Sitipedia article with subheads like "Fangs vs. Large Incisors: How to Differentiate," "Bat Training 101," and "Best Garlic Body Lotions."

Bay Area teen Lanie Vendriak says the Sitipedia article has been a literal lifesaver. "I can't tell you how many times I thought I was babysitting regular kids, and it turned out they were vampires!" she said.

"I don't get it," Gabby said when she finished the last clipping.

"Inaccurate," Edwina declared. "You're a highly intelligent girl who just had a close encounter with a slug-child and a talking cat. You might be struggling with several layers of denial, but you most certainly *do* 'get it.'"

Edwina was right. Everything Gabby had seen and

read pointed to only one answer. "Philip *is* an alien," Gabby admitted. It felt weird to say it out loud, but it also felt right. "And so are his parents and Vondlejax."

"Very good," Edwina said. "Anything else?"

"Well"—Gabby thought about the articles—"they can't be the only ones, because all those articles were about other aliens from years ago until now, and from different places all over the country. And the Sitipedia one says people are posting from all over the world. And *you* . . ." Gabby looked again at the logo and title, still glowing on the screen on the back of the limo seat. "You must work with A.L.I.E.N., the Association Linking Intergalactics and Earthlings as Neighbors."

"See? You *do* have a talent for deductive reasoning," Edwina noted. "Despite what your math teacher said on your last report card."

"You read my report card?" Gabby asked.

"As you've surmised," Edwina continued, "aliens have been living among us for a very long time. And as you've seen for yourself, while human beings have many points in their favor, accepting things they don't understand is not among them."

Something clicked in Gabby's head. "When you call human beings 'they,'" she asked, "is that because—"

"This is problematic, given that most aliens come in

peace, and they would much prefer *not* to be hunted down and dissected," Edwina said, once again ignoring Gabby's interruption. Gabby noticed that this time, "they" referred to the aliens. So much for clues about Edwina's identity.

"That's where my associates and I come in," Edwina said. "We at A.L.I.E.N. make it our business to maintain peaceful human–intergalactic-being integration. When mishaps occur, we make sure they're perceived as flights of fancy, tricks of the light, or easily dismissible mythologies."

"Like the vampires," Gabby said. "So . . . are *all* monsters actually aliens? Mummies and zombies and werewolves and—"

"And leprechauns and centaurs and fairies and all number of creatures who have disguised themselves so well through the centuries that they haven't inspired any stories about them at all, yes. Overall, we at A.L.I.E.N. are quite proud of our record of success. With one notable exception. Can you guess what it is?"

Gabby looked down at Edwina's laptop and scrolled again through the headlines. She remembered how eager John and Lisa were to hire her.

"Babysitting?" she asked.

Edwina nodded. "It has been a challenge. Time and again mishaps like the ones in those articles threatened to expose the secret we've worked so very hard to contain. The situation has become so dangerous that we had to declare all intergalactic children officially Unsittable."

"Unsittable?" Gabby echoed. "But that's horrible. Every kid is sittable."

"Only given the right sitter," Edwina said. She looked into the rearview mirror and fixed Gabby with a pointed stare.

"Me?"

"You can't be everywhere at once, of course," Edwina said, "and we recognize you have other clients and responsibilities. But if you do this, if you're willing to keep our secrets and join our cause, I assure you that you'll be doing a great service to families very much in need of your talents. And of course, you'll be rewarded most handsomely."

"When you say 'keep your secrets' . . ."

"From everyone," Edwina stated. "That's nonnegotiable."

Gabby flopped back in her seat and thought. *Unsittable* was a terrible thing to call a kid, especially a kid as great as Philip. And she'd made John and Lisa so happy just by spending ten minutes with him. There must be all kinds of families just like them, and Gabby could make them just as happy. Lying to her own family would be awful, but Edwina had already promised four times her hourly rate. With that kind of money coming in on a regular basis, Gabby could do more than just help out at home, she could . . .

She almost couldn't think it out loud. It seemed so selfish, especially when she and Alice and Carmen had to consider car payments and school clothes and college funds. . . .

But with the kind of money Edwina was talking about, Gabby could afford to be a little selfish. No, not selfish. Aspirational. She could give her family everything they needed and still have enough to pursue a dream she'd held close since Maestro Jenkins first heard her play and suggested it.

R.A.M.A. The Royal Academy for the Musical Arts, in London. The finest college for anyone wanting a career in music. Ninety percent of its graduates moved immediately to careers in professional orchestras, and every major philharmonic looked to R.A.M.A. to fill their ranks. Maestro Jenkins said that as a female French horn player Gabby was so unique that if she graduated from R.A.M.A. she could have her choice of the best orchestras in the world. The Berlin Philharmonic, the Royal Concertgebouw Orchestra in Amsterdam, the London Symphony Orchestra, the New York Philharmonic . . . Maestro Jenkins said they'd all fight for the honor of having her on their stage.

It sounded like a dream, and Gabby had immediately looked up the school online and discovered it could *only* be a dream. R.A.M.A.'s tuition was more than Alice made in a year. Even with aid and scholarships, Gabby would have to find money for travel and expenses and textbooks. There was just no way.

But college was six years from now. If she started working for Edwina today and set aside a little each month, she could have enough for R.A.M.A. She could take care of Alice and Carmen and still make her dreams come true. Plus, she'd be there for families like Philip's, who needed her desperately.

All that good had to outweigh the bad of keeping secrets, right?

Gabby put her business face on and leaned forward in her seat. "Here's the deal," she said. "My sister handles my books, so you'll need to set up a payment plan with her. And if you're really paying me four times my rate, we'll have to give her some kind of reason why."

"Unnecessary," Edwina said. "A.L.I.E.N. will deposit your fees in a special account to which you'll have easy access. When it grows to a tidy enough sum, we'll create a very old and very dead long-lost relative who left the family an annuity in his will. Checks will come to your house, at which point your sister can deal with them as she sees fit."

"Okay, good, good." Gabby chewed on her lip as her mind danced through all the other complications. "That leaves scheduling. I do that through Carmen, too, but it's not like you can call and say, 'It's Edwina from A.L.I.E.N.' So here's what I'm thinking—how about we set up a secret code, so when she tells me about the job I know it's actually you? Like you could use the word 'vanilla.' Or 'salamander.'"

Or always use a last name with an umlaut—"

"We know where to find you," Edwina cut her off, "and we're well aware of your schedule. When we need you, we'll be in touch. That is, if you're saying yes."

Gabby imagined her mom throwing flour in the air and dancing in the flurries when she heard about the long-lost relative's will. She imagined Carmen raising her eyebrow in a grand show of amazement at their new, full bank account. She imagined herself in ten years, standing proudly in a navy blue cap and gown as she accepted her diploma from R.A.M.A. She imagined the families she'd helped cheering her from the audience, stray tentacles accidentally popping loose as they applauded and wiped away grateful tears.

Gabby took a deep breath. There was only one response, but saying it out loud still felt momentous, like everything in her life was about to change.

"Yes," she said. "I'll do it."

Edwina smiled. "Then by the power vested in me by the Association Linking Intergalactics and Earthlings as Neighbors, I hereby declare you, Gabby Duran, Associate 4118-25125A: Sitter to the Unsittables."

chapter
FIVE

*g*abby spent the rest of the ride in silence, her mind too filled with wonder to speak. When the limo pulled up in front of her house, Gabby knew that for appearances' sake, she should fly out like she always did after a job. But the occasion felt too monumental for that.

"Thank you for the ride, Edwina," she said formally. "And of course for the opportunity."

Edwina didn't respond. She simply looked at Gabby in the rearview mirror.

"It was great meeting you," Gabby offered.

She waited for Edwina to tell her it was great meeting her, too. It didn't happen.

"O-kay, then. So I'll just . . ." She reached for the door handle, then thought better of it. "Do you have a cell phone or anything? In case I wake up tomorrow with all kinds of questions I forgot to think of, and—"

Edwina pressed a button on the console. Gabby's door popped open.

"Right," Gabby said. "You'll find me."

She grabbed her purple knapsack and slid out of the limo, which screeched away the second she shut the door. Across the street, Madison was again playing flute in the living room. She wondered if Maestro Jenkins had told her about R.A.M.A., too. Maybe they'd end up there together. Maybe by then, she and Madison would be friends. Maybe they'd be roommates even. And after graduation they'd end up in the same orchestra and they'd tell funny stories to reporters about their early days as bitter rivals at Brensville Middle School.

Madison stopped playing and glanced out her window. Gabby thought she was pretty invisible on the darkened street, but Madison locked eyes with her, then shook her head with a smug smile.

The message was clear. *I practiced, you didn't. I win, you lose.*

Okay, so maybe they wouldn't be R.A.M.A. roommates. Gabby turned and darted inside her house, clomping extra loud so it might seem like she ran in as usual. "Mom? Car?" she called.

"Down here, sweetie!" Alice answered.

Gabby trotted downstairs to the TV room. Alice was sprawled on the overstuffed couch, decompressing to the drone of Food Network. She still wore her stained It's All Relativity apron from the Greek-Italian-Cajun themed Diwali luncheon. Carmen hovered over the Puzzle Place—an old behemoth of a dining room table the Durans had found at a secondhand store, refinished, and turned into a home for Carmen's favorite hobby: impossibly complicated jigsaw puzzles.

"How were the triplets?" Alice asked.

For a second, Gabby had no idea who she meant. John, Lisa, and Philip?

"Oh, you mean Ali, Lia, and Ila!" Gabby remembered, reaching back to what seemed like ages ago. "They were great!"

Carmen looked up from her puzzle. "You sound weird."

"And the flight?" Alice asked. "You said there was trouble, but Carmen checked that Web site that tracks all the planes, and it said the flight left and arrived right on time."

"Really?" Gabby squeaked. Her palms tickled with sweat. "Oh, that's because the trouble was after we landed. Long time on the runway. Is it getting hot in here?" She tugged on her shirt and flapped her arms like chicken wings to get a breeze on her suddenly swampy torso.

"You're acting weird, too," Carmen said.

"Oh yeah?" Gabby countered. "Weirder than choosing a jigsaw puzzle that's a giant math problem?"

"It's a twenty-five thousand piece artistic exploration of pi, taken to two thousand digits," Carmen shot back.

"If the pie was taken to two thousand *flavors*, that would be normal," Gabby said.

"But it wouldn't make sense," Carmen said, scrunching her face. "Pi's a number. It doesn't come in flavors."

"Pie-with-an-e does," Alice said, "and I happen to have a lemon meringue in the fridge. Gabby, why don't you slice some for us?"

That was Alice's favorite way of handling it when the girls bickered: separation, ideally combined with sweets. Gabby tromped back upstairs and sliced three wedges of the pie. She made Carmen's extra-large as an apology. She hadn't really meant to pick on her sister; she just panicked when Car caught her acting strange. If Gabby was going to be a top-secret associate for a covert governmental agency, she had to get better at this lying thing. Snapping at Carmen all the time wouldn't work, and if she kept sweating this much every time she stretched the truth, she'd end her first week as a pile of salt and curls.

"You only have two pieces," Alice said when Gabby went downstairs and handed her and Carmen each a plate. "Aren't you having any?"

"Mine's in the kitchen. I thought I'd bring it upstairs and have it while I practice." Translation: *I can't be around you without letting you know I'm keeping a secret.*

"Play loud," Carmen said. "I like hearing you."

Carmen wasn't even looking at Gabby—her full attention was on the puzzle—but Gabby felt like her sister had just given her a huge hug. "Thanks, Car." She kissed her sister on top of her head, and even though Carmen wiped the kiss off like it was bird poop, Gabby swore she saw a hint of a smile.

"My turn," Alice said, holding out her arms.

When Gabby came closer for a hug, Alice held her at arm's length. "You look so much like your father sometimes, it's crazy."

"You think?"

Gabby was only two when her dad died, and he'd been deployed six months before that. She didn't really remember him, and she couldn't see the resemblance in pictures, but Alice swore they had the exact same bright blue eyes and freckles; and pre-army, when her dad's hair had been long, Alice said it had been just as curly as Gabby's.

Alice ruffled Gabby's curls, then pulled her in for a hug. Gabby could smell the tandoori spices still lingering on her mom's clothes. "Don't stay up too late practicing, baby," Alice said. "It's a school night. Carmen and I are going to bed soon, too."

Gabby promised, then bounced up to the kitchen, grabbed her slice of pie, and carried it to her room. After scarfing two huge bites, she opened her French horn case and tried to practice Friday afternoon's solo. She made it through once, playing extra loud for Carmen's benefit, but she wasn't feeling the notes. All she could think about were aliens.

They were real. They lived all around us. She had just personally met four of them. Maybe five; the jury was still out on Edwina. They were everywhere, hidden in plain sight. People Gabby knew could be aliens. People like Ronnie, the bus driver who always shouted, even when she was right in front of you. Or the woman at Alice's favorite bakery who hated kids but loved dogs. Maybe she came from a planet where everyone was fluffy with a tail, so the dogs made her feel at home.

Or maybe *Madison* was an alien. Maybe that's how she could see Gabby in the darkness earlier. Maybe she had creepy mind-tweaking powers, which forced Maestro Jenkins to love her music but messed with her own brain and made it impossible for her to be nice to Gabby, no matter how nice

Gabby was to her.

Gabby put away her horn, yanked her phone out of her purple knapsack, and leaped over a pile of dirty laundry to flop on the bed and call Zee. Zee would love this. If Gabby told her there were aliens around, she'd dive in and analyze every detail about every person in their lives until she knew for sure who was earthling and who was intergalactic. It'd be just like the time Gabby found the anonymous "I love you, Gabby Duran" letter in her fifth-grade locker, and Zee went full forensics, dissecting speech patterns, gestures, habits, and daily routines of everyone who had even the remotest contact with Gabby, including some who might have sent the note as a prank. When the culprit turned out to be Wally Ramone, a fourth-grade trumpet player whose lips were always pursed into playing position, Gabby's disappointment was completely overshadowed by her awe of Zee's skills. The clue that closed the case? Turkey jerky. It was Wally's favorite snack. He ate it constantly, and both he and the letter carried its distinctive odor.

Zee would love Gabby's latest mystery even more, but Gabby realized there was no way she could tell her. She'd promised Edwina. If she spilled, she broke the rules, and she wouldn't be allowed to babysit for A.L.I.E.N. No sitting, no money, no helping her family, no R.A.M.A. Plus, kids like Philip would go back to being "Unsittable."

Gabby stopped the call before she even finished dialing. She rolled onto her stomach and screamed into her comforter.

This was impossible. She needed something to distract her.

Could she call Satchel? Even though his mom and Alice had drifted apart a little since their maternity ward room-mate days, years of shared playdates, shared birthday parties, and embarrassing-to-look-at-the-videos-now shared baths had sealed their deal. Gabby and Satchel were one hundred percent brother and sister, even if they did have different houses and different parents. Gabby knew him as well as she knew herself, and knew exactly what he'd be doing right now. It was nine at night on a Sunday, so he'd have just fin-ished making bike deliveries for his uncle Gio's restaurant. He'd answer if Gabby called, and there'd be no danger of her talking about A.L.I.E.N. because, unlike Zee, he'd lose it and Gabby would never freak him out that way. But what else could Gabby talk about? A.L.I.E.N. was the only thing on her mind.

She turned off her phone and plugged it in. Better to just go to sleep and deal with everything in the morning. She got ready for bed, crawled under the covers . . .

. . . and didn't wake up until she felt the oozing drool of a strange alien beast dripping onto her face.

"Philip!" she cried as she bolted upright in bed.

It wasn't Philip. It wasn't even an alien. It was that Zee-rigged pitcher of water that doused Gabby every time she pressed the snooze button a third time. As always, she gathered her soaking sheets for the dryer, then got dressed and ready for school and joined Alice and Carmen in the kitchen. Both of them were well into plates of chicken tikka masala, left over from yesterday's brunch. Gabby stared at the heap of chunky yellow-orange goo in front of her own chair and wondered, Could her own mother be an alien? It would explain her penchant for serving decidedly un-breakfasty foods at breakfast.

"Not in the mood for leftovers?" Alice said. "I can make you something else."

"No, it's not that," Gabby said quickly, shaking off the ridiculous idea. "This looks great. I was just thinking about stuff. What's my schedule like this week, Car?"

Between bites, Carmen opened one of her black binders. "Today the Graces, tomorrow the Hayses, Wednesday the Vitaris twins, Thursday the Hayses again," she rattled off. "Friday we left open for the concert."

Interesting. All regulars. Nothing that sounded like code for Edwina.

Then again, Gabby had only been named Sitter to the Unsittables yesterday. It was crazy to think she'd be booked already.

Except John and Lisa seemed like they'd have hired Gabby immediately.

"Do we have anyone unusual coming up in the next few weeks?" Gabby asked. "Anyone . . . I don't know . . . unique?"

Carmen flipped through the book. "Rajit Jethani plays banjo. That's unique. The Cody sisters' grandmother just turned a hundred and two, which is very unique. Adelia Montrose has a dog that won the Westminster Kennel Club's Best in Show. Renee Vel—"

"Got it, thanks." Gabby cut her off before Carmen went through each standout quirk of every single client in the book.

Carmen's watch beeped and she shut the binder. "Time to go," she said. "Bus arrives in three minutes, thirty-nine seconds."

This, Carmen had calculated, was the exact amount of time it took for her and Gabby to put on their coats, gather their bookbags and Gabby's instrument, and get to the stop at the corner. Madison Murray, whose sense of timing was nowhere near as impeccable as Carmen's, was already waiting when they arrived.

"Hi, Madison!"

Gabby said it brightly, but subtly narrowed her eyes, trying to peer through Madison's skin for signs of alien sluginess.

"What are you doing with your face?" Carmen asked. "You look like you smell something bad."

"Carmen! Cut it out. I don't look like that at all." Gabby turned to Madison. "Sorry about that. Don't know what she was talking about."

She offered Madison a chummy laugh. Madison didn't join in. Instead she said, "I noticed the light in your bedroom window was out by ten last night. I was up playing my flute until midnight, then listened to the concerto on headphones, so I'd get extra practice in my sleep. You should probably just go ahead and tell Maestro Jenkins you don't want Friday's solo. It'll save you the suspense of waiting until he gives it to me."

The bus pulled up before Gabby could respond. When Madison turned around to board, Gabby studied her back for any signs of a hidden tail.

"Good morning, girls!" Ronnie the bus driver screamed unnecessarily as they climbed inside. Were her alien ears unable to gauge how loud she was?

Gabby turned down the aisle and stopped in her tracks. The seats were filled with elementary and middle schoolers laughing, shouting, throwing things, zoning out to headphones, bent over homework, or staring out the window. Were they all human? Had she been riding the bus with aliens all her life? How would she know?

"Butts in seats, or I can't move the bus!" Ronnie cried in her earsplitting bellow.

Gabby quickly slipped into an empty bench a short walk down the aisle, leaving Carmen the only bench she'd accept, the one right behind Ronnie's chair. Gabby took a deep breath and let it out slowly. She had to stop thinking about what happened last night. She couldn't function like this.

Music would help. Gabby pulled out her phone and earbuds, scrolled to her recording of Friday afternoon's concerto, hunkered down in her seat, closed her eyes, and let the notes fill her head and take her away from everything.

Everything except a sharp pain in her shin. An alien attack?

"Wake up, Gabby," Carmen said. She stood in the aisle next to Gabby's bench. "You fell asleep. We're at your school."

"Oh," Gabby said, rubbing the spot on her leg Carmen had kicked. "Thanks. I think."

Carmen smirked slightly as she went back to her own bench, and Gabby limped herself, her purple knapsack, and her French horn case off the bus.

The minute she hit the curb, a streak of blue and yellow whizzed by, shouting her name.

"Zee!" Gabby happily replied. She raced after her, the knapsack and French horn galumphing against her body with each step.

Stephanie Ziebeck, a.k.a. Zee, rode to school on a motorized skateboard she'd tricked out herself. Hence the super-streak speeds. The super-streak colors came from her blue overalls, every pair of which had a multitude of pockets for gadgets and devices, and her yellow-blond hair, with the almost-equally-multitudinous braids that whipped behind her as she rode.

Gabby caught up with Zee as Zee toe-flipped her skateboard and caught it under her arm.

"Did it finally work?" Zee asked. She was referring, as she did every morning, to the pitcher of water she'd rigged to Gabby's alarm.

"Pavlov totally would have had me put to sleep," Gabby admitted.

"You're killing me," Zee said. She threw her non-skateboard-holding arm around Gabby's shoulders, and they walked into Brensville Middle School. "Come with me, Gabs," she said. "I worked up something new for the L-Man over the weekend."

The L-Man was Ellerbee, the school janitor. His office was right across from the office of the principal. In the first week of school, Zee had rigged some pencils, rubber bands, and a tiny engine into a flying drone that she let loose in the middle of English. She got sent to Tate's, but while she was waiting she saw Ellerbee struggling with a broken vacuum cleaner. Zee fixed it, and the two became friendly. Apparently, Ellerbee's son, who now lived pretty far away and never visited, had been into robotics when he was Zee's age, so Ellerbee understood Zee's dreams of building a bot worthy of a national championship. He also understood why Zee wanted nothing to do with the school's official robotics team, which was manned by Principal Tate. Principal Tate was a man who believed in following rules no matter what, even when those rules sucked the creative life out of something. Ellerbee's son had been more like Zee, and Ellerbee loved sharing his son's old tricks and ideas with her. In return, Zee tried to use her skills to make his job a little easier.

"ZZ Top! Gabby MacGregor!" Ellerbee cried in his thick Scottish accent as he rolled back in his chair. Unlike the principal's palace across the way, Ellerbee's office was little more than a glorified walk-in closet. Shelves crammed with squeeze bottles of cleanser, rags, and buckets lined the walls, while large vacuums, mops, brooms, and buffers crowded the floor. Ellerbee's desk was actually a repurposed lower shelf. His roller chair barely fit beneath it.

"Good to see ya, L-Man!" Zee said.

"Hi, Ellerbee," Gabby added with a smile. She looked at Ellerbee's framed picture of his hometown—the one he always kept on his desk. He'd told Zee he hadn't been back to Ayr in forty-five years, but he still missed it. Gabby wondered if Philip's family and Vondlejax felt the same way about their home planets.

"Totally hooked you up," Zee said. Her backpack was already on the ground, and she dug inside until she pulled out what looked like foot clips for skis. "Still got the Roombas I juiced for you?"

"Aye, taking up space, I'm afraid," Ellerbee said. He gestured to a pair of round robotic vacuum cleaners Zee had found at a secondhand store. She'd fixed them and rigged them with jet power, so Ellerbee could let them loose and have them finish his work in record time. Unfortunately, the first time he tried one, it slammed into a shelving unit in the science room and spilled sulfuric acid all over the floor. Zee had wanted to pay for the damages herself, but Ellerbee wouldn't let her. He had Tate dock it from his paycheck.

"It's a Newton thing," Zee said as she used the tools in her overalls to tinker with the Roombas and clips. "An object in motion stays in motion unless acted upon by an external force. *You*, L-Man, will be that external force." She stood back and gestured to her creation. "I call it . . . the Shoomba."

Ellerbee cautiously slipped his feet into the shoelike clamps that were now secured onto the robot vacuums. "You're asking me to ride on these, lassie?"

Zee nodded. "You lean to steer. Try it!"

"Not with you here, ZZ," Ellerbee chuckled. "Don't want

you to get in trouble if things fly south. You get ready for class, and I'll let you know how they work."

He and Zee exchanged fist bumps, he waved to Gabby, then the two girls trooped toward their lockers. "Must be hard for Ellerbee," Gabby said as they walked, "living so far away from home."

"I guess," Zee said.

Gabby was talking about the janitor, but she was *thinking* about Philip and his family and Vondlejax. And it was really hard not to talk about them out loud to Zee.

"Did you know they call people who live in this country but aren't from here 'aliens'?" Gabby asked.

Zee scrunched up her face. "Of course I know that. Same thing they call creatures from outer space."

"Right . . . only there's no such thing as *space* aliens," Gabby said quickly.

"'Course there is," Zee said as they hit their lockers and tucked the French horn and skateboard into the deep cubbies beneath.

Gabby's blue eyes widened as she gaped at her best friend. "You know about them?"

"Sure," Zee said. "With all the billions of planets in the universe, it only makes sense there's alien life somewhere. Maybe even as close as Jupiter's moon Europa. Scientists say the oceans there might support life. Pretty cool, right?" Zee cocked her head, flopping her braids to the side. "Why are we talking about this?"

Gabby's skin prickled. "What do you mean? You're the one who brought up space aliens." She said it a little louder in case any were listening. "I did *not* bring up space aliens."

Zee frowned and studied Gabby, but before she could say anything, another voice called their names.

"Gabby! Zee!"

It was Satchel. He pinballed down the hall, his lanky body ricocheting off every circled-up clique until he reached the girls. "What's up?"

"Gabby's hiding something from me," Zee told him.

"No way! She is?"

"I'm not!" Gabby balked.

"Check it out," Zee said, beckoning Satchel closer. "She's talking too loud, she's blushing, and if you look close, you can see little beads of sweat on her forehead and upper lip."

"Lemme see," Satchel said. His dark hair flopped in his face as he leaned close to investigate. "Oh yeah! Look at that. It's like a little sweat mustache!"

"You guys, cut it out!" Gabby cried, backing away. "I'm not hiding anything."

"See how she's not looking us in the eye?" Zee said. "People do that when they're not telling the truth. And check her arms, flat at her side. When you feel weird about lying, you want to take up as little space as possible."

"I knew that!" Satchel exclaimed. "Gabby and I saw it in *Decimator Two*, when the hijacker was lying to Commando Adam Dent and he totally saw right through it! Oh snap, Gabby, you saw him yesterday, right? Was he on the set? Was it a new *Decimator*? What's it about? I know you're going to say you can't tell me, but you totally have to tell me!"

"I can't say for sure it's a *Decimator*, but I can tell you this," Gabby began, then gave him a few tiny details she knew he'd love. It was more than she'd usually share, but she was anxious to steer the conversation away from aliens and lies. Then the bell rang, and she and Zee split from Satchel to climb the two flights of stairs to Mr. Shamberg's English class. The lecture was about Edgar Allan Poe's "The Tell-Tale Heart," and Gabby realized she was a lot like the protagonist of the story. No, she hadn't killed anyone and hidden them under the floorboards, but she did have a secret she couldn't tell, and she was letting it haunt her. If Gabby wanted a better ending than the guy in the story, she had to get it together.

"Sorry I was acting weird before," she told Zee when class ended. "I think I'm just freaked about the concert Friday. I worked this weekend, so I didn't practice as much as Madison."

"But you're better than Madison," Zee said, "so you don't

have to practice as much."

It wasn't really true, Gabby knew. The French horn was one of the hardest instruments in the orchestra and even the best players needed lots of practice, but it was nice of Zee to say. And thinking about the solo definitely helped take Gabby's mind off her big secret. By lunchtime all she wanted to do was rehearse, so the second she finished eating, she excused herself from Satchel and Zee, grabbed her instrument, and ran down two flights of stairs to the music department practice rooms to play. After school, a job sitting one of her regulars, dinner, and homework, she was at the horn again, and played until *after* Madison's bedroom light went out across the street.

By morning, Gabby was totally herself again. She did ask Carmen if any new and unusual clients had contacted her, but no one had. Days passed, and not a single person asked for Gabby's babysitting services who wasn't a regular or referred by a regular. Gabby didn't see Edwina anymore, she didn't see any pets get up on their hind legs and talk, and no one shed their skin to reveal a body of gelatinous ooze.

Honestly, by the time Gabby sat in Mr. Shamberg's English class Friday morning, she was sure the entire Edwina/Philip/John/Lisa/Vondlejax experience was only a crazy dream she'd had on the way home from babysitting the triplets. Her mind was far more occupied by the concert. It was today after school, only a few hours away, and of course Maestro Jenkins still hadn't awarded the solo. Gabby had worked so hard all week that, even though she'd be a good sport, she'd be heartbroken if Madison got it instead of her.

That's what she was thinking about when a flutter of movement outside caught her eye, and she nearly screamed out loud.

Edwina's face, half hidden among the leaves of a tree, was framed in the window.

The *third floor* window.

chapter SIX

*g*abby tried to swallow but choked on her own saliva. She wondered if anyone had ever needed the Heimlich for what was basically a spitball.

"May I be excused?" she coughed out.

Mr. Shamberg let her go, so she grabbed her purple knapsack, ignored Zee's curious look, and raced downstairs. She avoided Ellerbee and the scattered students with free periods roaming the halls, zoomed out of the building, ran to the tree outside her English class, and looked up, fully expecting to see Edwina floating in midair.

No. Not floating. She couldn't have been floating. She

must have been sitting on a branch. She must have climbed the tree and sat on a branch.

Except the lowest branches were twenty feet off the ground. Edwina couldn't have climbed.

Gabby squinted and peered into the leaves. "Edwina!" she hissed.

No answer. Gabby saw no sign of her either. No black duster. No black wool pants. No chunky black shoes. No shock of white hair around a crimped face.

Nothing.

Was Gabby dreaming again? Did she fall asleep in class?

No. Impossible. She *saw* Edwina. She did.

Heart still pounding from the sprint downstairs, Gabby jumped to get a slightly closer look into the tree's high canopy of branches and leaves. She backpedaled to take in the entire roof of the school. Could Edwina have jumped up there?

She couldn't have. Of course she couldn't have. This was ridiculous. The stress about the solo clearly had Gabby's mind playing tricks on her. As the adrenaline drained from her body she flopped down onto the grass . . .

. . . and noticed a car idling under some trees across the street.

No, not a car. A limousine.

And suddenly she knew without a doubt that it had all been true.

She was a bit surprised, though, that Edwina was back in a limo. She'd assumed the first time it was a matter of camouflage. Gabby had expected a limo to pick her up after sitting the triplets. A limo at Brensville Middle School stood out like a zit on Picture Day.

Apparently, Edwina just liked to travel in style.

Gabby made her way to the limo and peered into the front seat. It was empty. She opened the back door.

Edwina was there, sitting ramrod straight as always, white hair in the severe bun that added two inches to her height. Every bit of her seemed to reach for the sky: the bun, her posture, her dangerously arched brows, the tip of her aristocratic nose. Even her wrinkles seemed angled upward in a pose of superiority.

"My, aren't you dressed like a penguin today," Edwina remarked.

Gabby looked down at herself. "Concert day," she explained. "Black skirt and tights and white blouse. My mom had this black velvet ribbon she wanted me to put in my hair, but I always feel so weird and constricted with my curls pulled back and I—"

"I was making an observation, not looking for a treatise," Edwina said in her clipped voice. "Please, get in and close the door."

Abashed, Gabby did as she was told. She pushed aside

one of several black square throw pillows, so she could slip onto the bench seat across from Edwina's. Then she placed her purple knapsack on the floor at her feet, just like Edwina had done with her own black bag. It was dimmer inside the car than outdoors, and if Gabby squeezed her eyes the littlest bit, Edwina's all-black clothing melded into the upholstery, so she looked like a ghostly head floating in nothingness.

"I'm really glad you came," Gabby said. "I mean, the *way* you came was a little disturbing, but still. I was starting to think I'd imagined everything, you know?" She smiled her most infectious smile.

Edwina didn't return it.

"I *don't* know," Edwina said. "I tend to trust my senses. It's a wiser way to live."

Gabby felt her mouth swell to accommodate her foot. She never had trouble talking to anyone, but chatting with Edwina was like walking a tightrope.

"I have a job for you," Edwina said.

Gabby's heart gave a hopeful little leap. "With Philip and his family?"

"Not this time. Your charge in this case is a little girl named what."

Edwina's coal-dark eyes bore into her. Was Gabby supposed to know the answer?

"Um . . . I'm not sure," she stammered.

"Not sure of what?" Edwina asked.

"Of the little girl's name."

"What."

"The little girl's name!" Gabby said louder. "I'm not sure of it!"

"The little girl's name is what."

"That's just it," Gabby said. "I don't know."

"You don't know *what*?"

"The little girl's name!"

"It is *WHAT*."

"I can't tell you what it is!" Gabby cried. "You haven't told me!"

Edwina closed her eyes and took a deep breath. "The little girl's name . . . is what."

Gabby opened her mouth to object, but Edwina held out a palm. "W-U-T-T," she spelled. "Wutt. *That's* the little girl's name."

"Wutt?" Gabby echoed.

"The little girl's name," Edwina raised her voice. "*Wutt* is what it is!"

"No, no, I get that now," Gabby assured her. "I just meant . . . really?"

"It's quite beautiful in her own language, I assure you."

"I see," Gabby mused. "Then, great! I'm in. When do I sit

for her? I can tell Carmen tonight and she can work it into the sched—"

Edwina picked up one of the throw pillows and thrust it in Gabby's face. "You sit today."

"*WHAT?!?!*" Gabby cried.

Instantly, the pillow folded out of itself and became a miniature-size girl with long red hair, giant eyes, and an enormous mouth, which opened in a high screeching shriek. Gabby shrieked back at the creature she suddenly held in her hands, then dropped it to the floor, where it scurried behind the bag at Edwina's legs and promptly folded itself back into a throw pillow.

"What *was* that?" Gabby gasped.

"*Yes,*" Edwina snapped, reaching down to pat the pillow gently on its corner.

"Yes, *wha*—" Gabby began, but caught herself as she realized. "Oh . . . what *was* that. I mean, *Wutt* was *that*. That was Wutt."

"Indeed," Edwina scolded. "And I assumed after Philip you'd handle the metamorphosis far more professionally. Now you've frightened the child."

Gabby blushed. "I'm so sorry." She pushed herself off the seat and onto the floor. She wanted to look Wutt in the eye and apologize to her directly, but she wasn't sure which part of the pillow was the girl's face. Or even her head. She opted for an area near the corner Edwina had patted and leaned in close.

"Hi, Wutt. I'm Gabby. I'm so sorry I scared you. I didn't even realize you were here, and then you popped out and screamed like that . . . I guess it kind of took me by surprise."

"Took you by surprise?" Edwina sniffed. "Of course she screamed. You might scream, too, if someone hollered your name into your face."

"Hollered her . . . ?" Gabby replayed the moment in her mind and realized she'd done just that. Her face grew even redder until it matched Wutt's curls. Or what would have been Wutt's curls if the girl weren't currently slipcovered.

"Can we start over?" Gabby asked the pillow. "I'm Gabby Duran, and I'm really happy to meet you. I even have something you might like. Want to see?"

The pillow didn't respond, but Gabby pulled over her purple knapsack anyway and dug around for one of the tiny treasures she always kept on hand, just in case. She found a pink pencil-top eraser decorated to look like a puppy.

"See?" Gabby showed the pillow. "It's an eraser, but I glued on little google eyes and a tiny bead nose and little felt ears. He can still rub away pencil marks, but he's also a pet, and *also* . . ." She slipped the eraser on the tip of her pinkie.

She waggled the finger as she continued in a deep doggy voice, "I'm a happy puppy puppet! I'm lots of things—kinda like you!"

Giggles erupted as the pillow unfolded itself back into a little girl. Wutt still hid behind Edwina's bag, but she was smiling now, and her large eyes danced.

"Hi, Wutt," Gabby said in her regular voice.

"What?"

"I said . . . Oh, wait—you were just repeating your name, weren't you?"

"Wutt," the little girl said happily. She climbed into Gabby's lap, then took the eraser pet off Gabby's pinkie tip and slipped it onto her own. It rode halfway down her finger.

Gabby was entranced watching Wutt play. The little girl was no bigger than a lawn gnome. Her red curls flowed all the way down to her rear end. The eyes Gabby thought earlier had popped wide in surprise really did take up half her face. Their long ovals were filled with endless shiny blackness. Her nose was tiny, barely more than twin paper cuts. Her skin was blue, with thin, darker blue lips that smiled happily as she played with the makeshift finger puppet. Her turquoise gums were unmarred by a single tooth.

She was adorable.

"So, Wutt," Gabby said gently, "you know how I said your name really, really loud before? That was just because I thought Edwina said I was babysitting you *today*. But I must have just misunderstood her. You see, she once told me she knows my schedule, which means she knows I'm way too busy to babysit today."

"Did you know, Wutt, that one of the surest signs of an underdeveloped civilization is when its members pretend to talk to one creature when their message is pointedly designed for another?" Edwina asked.

Gabby blushed yet again, then looked directly at Edwina. "I can't babysit Wutt today," she said. "I'm too bu—"

"Repeating yourself is just a waste of energy," Edwina said. "I *did* hear you." She consulted her tablet and swiped a few screens. "It's nine forty-five now, but we'll start your clock at nine A.M. You'll keep Wutt until midnight."

"*Wha—?!*" Gabby nearly exploded, but caught herself when the girl gave her a furrowed-brow look. Instead she smiled at the child and waved, then scooched along the car floor closer to Edwina and hissed up at her, "My bedtime's eleven on Friday nights."

"We'll pick her up, you won't need to worry about that...."

"I'm in school all day. I have class. I should be in class *right now*."

"Have her eat when you eat, that'll be fine. Anything should do. Just remember, she is gloogen-free."

"And right after school I have my concert with my possible solo and— Did you mean gluten-free?"

"Gloogen," Edwina affirmed. "Nasty little buggers from Sector 358.7. Pulverized for cheap protein by the laziest alien chefs."

Edwina shuddered, but Gabby laughed. "Don't worry," she told Edwina. "Chef Ernie might be lazy, but he's not an alien."

Edwina looked at Gabby meaningfully.

"Is he?" Gabby asked.

"Gloogen-free," Edwina reiterated. "And don't let her anywhere near broccolini. All that vitamin J. You know how it is. Hy-per."

"Vitamin . . . J?" Gabby asked. "Is that real?"

"Now I don't expect you to have any problems," Edwina continued, "but if you do, just keep in mind that Wutt is tenth in line to the throne of Flarknartia, a stunningly peaceful planet that has kept its harmonious place in the galaxy by following the old adage, 'If they knock down our tree, we knock down their forest. If they take over our city, we take over their continent. If they harm a hair on the head of the tenth in line to the throne, we explode their planet into tiny bits.'"

"I'm sorry—what?" Gabby gawped.

"Wutt?" the alien girl looked up in response.

"Exactly," Edwina said. "So that's that, then." She returned her tablet to her bag.

"When you say 'explode their planet into tiny bits,'" Gabby asked, "that's a euphemism, right?"

"Absolutely," Edwina replied. "We'd be blown into something far more like intergalactic dust. Out you go, then. I'll see you at midnight. Ready to go with Gabby, Wutt?"

Wutt looked up at Edwina as if the woman had just offered her a giant ice-cream sundae, perhaps one topped with broccolini. She squealed with delight, then leaped up and threw herself onto Gabby, attaching herself to the front of Gabby's fancy white blouse like a small baby gorilla.

"Wait, Edwina," Gabby said, "I've been trying to tell you. I have school today. I have a concert this afternoon. I'm not free."

"I hardly expect you to work for free, Gabby. I thought we'd established that."

"That's not what I mean. Even if I could keep Wutt with me, how could I keep her a secret?" Gabby put her hands over the little girl's ears. Or at least, she covered the spots on the sides of her head where her ears would be if they were oriented like a human being's. "She's wonderful, but she doesn't exactly blend in."

"You'd be surprised," Edwina said.

The back door of the limousine opened of its own volition.

"Go," Edwina said. "I have complete faith in you. And lovely homes on several outlying galaxies if things go terribly awry."

Gabby sighed heavily, then climbed out of the limousine, Wutt still clinging to her front. Yet the minute Gabby stood, she felt the girl release her grip. Instinctively, Gabby reached out to catch her . . . but what landed in her hands was a brown paper bag–covered textbook. The word MATH was inked on the front in big curlicue letters. Surrounding that, also in multicolored swirls, were a myriad of designs, inside jokes, and craftily hidden initials of particularly adorable middle school boys.

In short, it looked like any other sixth-grade girl's schoolbook.

"Wutt?" Gabby asked the book.

In answer, it lifted its cover several times and riffled its own pages. Gabby almost thought she could hear Wutt's giggle, though it might have just been the *fwit-fwit-fwit* of the paper.

Edwina was right. Gabby *was* surprised. She looked up to tell her so and was far less surprised to discover that the limousine had already disappeared.

chapter
SEVEN

*g*abby walked back toward the school slowly, staring down at the apparent math book in her hands.

"Normally, I put books in my knapsack," she mused to Wutt, "but with you that kind of feels wrong. Could you even breathe in there? Or maybe when you turn into something you're pretty much just like that thing, so breathing isn't really an issue. Or maybe breathing isn't an issue for you anyway. You know what, Wutt? When we get some time, I'd love to learn all about your planet."

"Are you talking to your math book?"

Disgust dripped from the all-too-familiar voice, and Gabby looked up to see Madison Murray right in front of her. Madison also wore concert dress, but her black skirt and white ruffled blouse looked so impeccable it made Gabby feel small and rumpled. Madison's arms were folded and her mouth curled, and Gabby found it highly annoying that even like that, she still looked really pretty.

"Talking to my math book?" Gabby laughed. "No! That would be ridiculous. More than ridiculous. Ridonculaciallous."

"That's not a word," Madison said. She pulled a small notebook and a pen from the purse slung over her shoulder. "I'm afraid as second period hall monitor it's my duty to write you up. One slip for loitering in the halls during class time, one for disturbing the peace by talking out loud to your textbook, and one for massacring the English language." Madison efficiently ripped off all three sheets, then handed them to Gabby. "I'll escort you to class to make sure you share these with your teacher. I do hope you don't get after-school detention. That would keep you away from the concert, and you can't possibly play a solo at a concert you don't even attend."

Madison's smug look made it very clear that she would *love* it if Gabby got detention.

"You really don't have to walk me to class, Madison. I promise I'll show Ms. Wilkins the notes."

"Citations," Madison clarified. "And of course I'll walk you. It's my duty."

Madison clip-clopped down the hall on low heels that matched her skirt and looked far more formal than Gabby's own black canvas sneakers. For Wutt's protection and her own sanity, Gabby stayed two steps behind Madison and willed Wutt to remain still.

Yet the longer Wutt *did* stay still, the more Gabby worried. *Should* the girl be flipping her pages? Was she all right? Did she need anything?

Gabby fell back a couple more steps and held the book to her mouth. "You okay, Wutt?" she whispered. "If you are, give your pages a little flutter."

Madison wheeled around as they arrived at Gabby's class . . . and saw Gabby with her lips pressed to the math book. Madison's eyes narrowed, and she again pulled out the notebook and pen. She scribbled a note, then ripped it off the pad and handed it to Gabby.

"'Citation for Inappropriate Public Display of Affection with a Textbook,'" Gabby read. "Is that even a thing?"

Madison pulled open the classroom door and cleared her throat loudly. Gabby's entire science class turned in their seats and stared. Satchel waved.

"Yes?" Ms. Wilkins's eyes bugged behind her glasses. "Bugged" was a general theme for Ms. Wilkins. In addition to the thick lenses that magnified her eyes and the endless creatures buzzing around the room's apiaries, ant farms, and terrariums, she always wore bug-themed clothing and jewelry. Today's theme was apparently cockroach.

"Ms. Wilkins," Madison said officiously, "since Gabby Duran is fifteen minutes late, I have delivered her to you personally, along with multiple citations for ill behavior in the halls. Gabby?"

Gabby held out the sheets of paper. Ms. Wilkins took them and crumpled them into a small ball. "Thank you so much, Madison," she chirped, "but I already received written permission for Gabby to arrive late." She tossed the citations in the trash.

Gabby would have enjoyed Madison's drop-jawed horror more if she had any idea how it happened. How did she get written permission to be late?

Ms. Wilkins leaned in close. "That was so kind of you to run to the flower store and have a bouquet sent to the hospital. I do hope your aunt Edwina gets better soon."

Gabby smiled. "Thank you. Yes, I hope so, too."

Now she could enjoy Madison's drop-jawed horror. At least for the two seconds before Madison turned and clip-clopped out of the room. Apparently, there were some side benefits to working for a secret government agency.

As it turned out, Gabby had arrived in science class just in time for a streaming video called *What Bugged the Dinosaurs: Exploring Mesozoic Insects.* Once the lights were out and everyone was either watching or pretending to watch while they snuck in texts, a chapter or two of a novel, or homework for other classes, Gabby cuddled Wutt-the-math-book against her chest, positioned—she hoped—so the little girl could enjoy the show and learn a little something about her adoptive planet.

The video ended at the same time the bell rang. Gabby tossed her knapsack over her shoulder, curled Wutt gently in the crook of her arm, and fell into step next to Satchel. As a percussionist, he was in concert dress too. He walked a little stiffly, constricted by the pressed black pants and button-down white starched shirt.

"How come you're holding the book?" he asked.

"You mean, '*Wutt*'s the book in my arms?'" Gabby teased.

"I know it's a book," Satchel said. "I just wondered why it's not in your bag."

"You mean, '*Wutt* has such a good reason to be outside my bag?'"

"I don't mean that at all," Satchel said. "Are you okay? What's your deal?"

"Yes," Gabby said proudly. "Today she is. Very much. See you at lunch!"

She peeled off into her math classroom, giggling over the perplexed look on Satchel's face. She felt a little bad for playing with him that way . . . but only a little. He'd panic if he knew the truth. Besides, she couldn't help feeling giddy. She had an *alien* in her arms! An alien *princess*: tenth in line to the throne, and *Gabby* got to watch over her. Not only was it an honor, it was the easiest babysitting job she'd ever had. It was also the most fulfilling. Gabby had been dubious about watching Wutt at school, but now she understood why Edwina wanted it this way. At school Gabby was able to both watch and educate Wutt. Already she'd taught her about Earth's early days; now she'd get to introduce her to geometry. The class was usually torture for Gabby, but she was so excited to share it with Wutt she practically skipped inside the classroom.

"Gabby!" Zee waved from the front row. She had her chair turned backward, so she straddled it with her arms crossed over its back.

Gabby almost didn't sit next to her. Keeping Wutt from Satchel was one thing, but for Zee meeting an alien would be a scientific revelation. How could Gabby deny that to her best friend?

Gabby sighed. Doing the right thing wasn't always easy, she told herself, but that didn't mean she should avoid it. She slipped into the seat next to Zee and gently placed the little-girl-in-math-book-form on the desk.

Zee leaned in close. "What happened in English today?

Why'd you run out?"

Gabby felt the words jump onto her tongue and rush her lips to fight their way out. She was dying to tell Zee the truth, so much that it hurt to keep it inside.

"Nothing!" Gabby said fake-cheerily through clenched teeth. "Stomach thing, that's all."

"Stomach thing," Zee said appraisingly, looking her friend up and down. "You do look pale and clammy."

Of course she did. She just told a flat-out lie to her best friend. She clamped her lips into a closed-mouth grimace and nodded.

"You sure you're okay?" Zee asked Gabby. "You seem . . ."

"Alien?" Gabby blurted.

She couldn't *tell* Zee what was going on, but if Zee *guessed* the truth, then it wouldn't be Gabby's fault the information got out. At least, that's how she looked at it.

Zee scrunched her face. "I was going to say 'weird,' but okay, 'alien' I guess."

"Yeah," Gabby said. "Alien. Good word. *Alien*. Very de-scriptive."

Gabby glanced pointedly at Wutt-the-math-book.

"Okay, something's up," Zee said. "Shoot."

"If I don't tell you, will you feel *alien*ated?"

"Alienated?"

"You won't think I'm violating your in*alien*able right to know?"

"What?"

"Yes, Wutt!" Gabby cried, holding up her math book. "Exactly!"

"Oh hey," Zee noted, "you re-covered your book." She plucked it from Gabby's hands to check it out. "'M.N. plus F.S.'? Who's that?"

"No one," Gabby said, grabbing back the book. "I mean . . . I don't know. I didn't write that. It's not my math book."

"Oh. Should we take it to the lost and found?"

"No!" Gabby shouted, hugging the book close. "She's mine! I mean, *it's* mine. The book is mine. When I said it wasn't, I meant the *cover* isn't mine."

Gabby was floundering now. She could feel the sweat bead on her face. Zee looked confused.

"You put someone else's cover on your math book?"

In response, a voice boomed from the back of the room.

"Did someone say *math book*?"

Gabby and Zee both turned to see a man built like Humpty Dumpty stride into the room. The hair that by all rights should have been on his head had migrated down to a well-manicured soul patch. He wore a purple cape.

"I have a theory about math books," he said as he surged

to the front of the room. "Math books are anathema to arithmetic. Allow me to introduce myself. I am Mr. Lau, and I am not only substituting for your math teacher, I am substituting for your old ways of thought, beginning with your thoughts on math books! Today we say this to math books: farewell!"

Before Gabby knew what was happening, Mr. Lau grabbed her book—grabbed *Wutt*—and hurled her to the ground. She smacked down with a loud *thwack*!

"No!" Gabby cried.

She tried to jump up, but Mister Lau leaned heavily on her desk, blocking her path.

"I know, intrepid student, it's hard to bid adieu to the box in which you've always lived. But today, in this class, we free our minds! Everyone, come to the front of the room and throw your book on the pile!"

"*NO!*" Gabby wailed. She did jump up this time, but Mr. Lau placed a hand on her shoulder and eased her back down in her chair.

"Stay strong, young scholar," he said. "Change can be hard, I know."

Already, the rest of the class was on their feet, books in hand. Gabby could only sit and watch helplessly as student after student—even her own best friend—slammed their books onto the floor, right on top of Wutt.

Gabby cringed. She bit her knuckles. She pounded her

fists on the desk. She yanked on chunks of her hair. She curled into a small ball and whimpered. She suffered through a lecture that had the rest of the class enraptured, while the image of Wutt's huge black eyes and toothless smile danced before her eyes.

The second the bell rang, Gabby raced to the stack of textbooks. She dug through them like a dog, pawing through the pile and hurling the discards behind her as she burrowed down. She vaguely heard the *bangs*, *thwacks*, and *ows* of books hitting desks, chairs, and shins, but none of that mattered. All she wanted was *her* book, and when she found it she snatched it and ran to a corner where she frantically inspected it for scratches or dents.

There were none.

Near tears, Gabby slid down the wall, hugging the book to her chest.

"So, um . . . we need to talk."

It was Zee. She stood in front of Gabby. Behind her, the entire math class spread in a tableau of flabbergasted bewilderment, every jaw on the floor.

chapter
EIGHT

*G*abby looked at the sea of her concerned—or just seriously freaked-out—classmates.

"We totally need to talk," she told Zee. "Later."

Gabby grabbed her purple knapsack, threw it over her shoulder, and raced out of the classroom at a full run, still clutching Wutt to her chest. She knew Zee wouldn't follow. Zee had Art, but Gabby had fourth period free, and unlike Madison Murray, her free periods weren't spent busting other people in the halls.

Gabby tore down the two flights of stairs to the music department. As she ran her phone rang.

Which was strange because she always turned it off before she left for school.

And it wasn't so much ringing as it was honking. This hideous *a-WOO-ga* sound that she would never in a million years assign to anything, and that would bring every faculty member running with detention slips if she didn't shut it up immediately.

Desperate as she was to make sure Wutt was okay, she had to stop the racket. She slowed to a walk and dug in her knapsack for the phone.

It was on and making that horrible sound, but nothing was on the screen except a little swirling wheel. That usually only happened when the phone had to shut itself down and restart. Was her phone broken? Even if it was, why was it making that noise?

Suddenly the sound stopped.

Edwina's face replaced the swirling wheel on the screen.

"Well hello, Ms. Duran," she said.

Gabby screamed and dropped the phone.

Edwina tsked. The phone had landed upside-down, so Gabby couldn't see her, but she could imagine the lowered lids, the thin-pressed lips, the head shaking almost imperceptibly in disapproval.

"Really, Gabby?" Edwina said once Gabby picked up the phone again. "Phone dropping? I honestly thought we'd moved beyond that kind of melodrama."

"What are you . . ." Gabby stammered. "How are you . . . How did you get in my phone?"

"The same way the tiny people got into your television set to act out your favorite shows," Edwina said drily.

"I didn't mean that," Gabby blushed. "I meant—"

"I'd love to answer all your questions, but unfortunately I have no desire to do so. I do, however, have news that's rather urgent and can only be delivered to you while you're alone, which is now."

Gabby looked around. It was true. Despite the way the phone had screamed, the stairwell was still empty.

"Can you hurry?" Gabby whispered. "I really need to do something."

"Something as in make sure you didn't bend, fold, spindle, or mutilate the tenth in line to the Flarknartian throne?"

Gabby's stomach sank to her feet. How did Edwina know? "Something like that," she admitted.

"Once a Flaknartian has assumed the shape of another object," Edwina said, "he or she can only be damaged if that object is rent into pieces or punctured clean through. Was Wutt torn apart or impaled?"

"No!" The very idea made Gabby nauseous.

"Then you have bigger things to worry about," Edwina noted. "It seems our anonymity was compromised.

Somewhere at your school is a member of the underground Group Eradicating Totally Objectionable Uninvited Trespassers, a.k.a. G.E.T. O.U.T."

"G.E.T. O.U.T?" Gabby scrunched her brows. "They're G.E.T. O.U.T. and you're A.L.I.E.N.? No offense, but for secret organizations you guys come up with really obvious names."

"It's not like we carry business cards," Edwina huffed. "At least, not anymore. But you're missing the point. G.E.T. O.U.T. is a rogue association helmed by an alien-obsessed paranoid named Hubert Houghton."

The image on the phone changed to one of a shadowy silhouette behind a closed window shade. That was replaced by a picture of a man walking outside in a large city. Gabby guessed it was the same man in the silhouette, but she couldn't tell. All she could see were thick-soled shoes, long pants, and a trench coat that covered his entire body. The man's face was hidden by a dark scarf, surgical mask, giant bug-eye sunglasses, and a wide-brimmed fedora. He walked hunched over, hands deep in his pockets. A final picture seemed plucked from a newscast. The name HUBERT HOUGHTON was written under an image so pixelated it was just scrambled color swirls.

"Are these pictures supposed to help me in any way?" Gabby asked.

"They prove a point," Edwina said as her face popped back onto Gabby's screen. "Hubert Houghton is a paranoid germaphobe, agoraphobe, and claustrophobe. To our knowledge, no one has ever seen his adult face. He rarely leaves his house, which is actually a skyscraper covering an entire city block of Manhattan. Houghton is convinced the world's problems stem from pollution. Not ecological pollution, but pollution of the human species by alien invaders. The man has fewer brain cells than a Jilkstarbriak Flusherflom, but billions of dollars in family money to fund what he feels is his moral imperative: the ejection and/or destruction of all extraterrestrials on Earth, as well as those who help them."

"Like you?"

"Like *you*. Our sources tell us G.E.T. O.U.T. suspects you're involved with us, and you're with an alien child. Should they become certain of this information, they will undoubtedly try to capture you, and quite likely kill you both."

"WHAT?!" Gabby wailed.

With a ta-da sounding flourish, the math book in Gabby's arms splayed back into a wild-haired little girl. She smiled wide and gave Gabby a huge hug.

"Ah, you see?" Edwina smiled. "I told you she was fine."

Gabby's head was spinning, and she was way too visible holding an alien in the middle of the stairwell. Keeping Wutt clutched close, she scampered down the rest of the stairs and raced through the halls until she got to the practice rooms: eight square rooms, each of which was outfitted with a piano, a music stand, posters illustrating all the instruments in a proper orchestra . . . and nothing else. They were the most private spots in all Brensville Middle School.

Gabby raced into the farthest practice room on the left, slammed herself and Wutt inside, then peered through the tiny door in the window to make sure no one was coming.

"Wutt?" Wutt asked, her giant eyes blinking curiously.

"It's cool," Gabby said. "We're alone. Let me just talk to Edwina a second. You can play with whatever you can find in the bag."

She set down both Wutt and her purple knapsack, then settled onto the piano bench and stared back into the phone.

The screen was blank.

"Edwina!" Gabby cried. She shook the phone. She pressed the button below the screen. She tapped madly at the glass, harder and harder. . . .

"Stop! Stop! You're giving me a headache!" Edwina grimaced as her face crackled back into view.

"You can feel it when I tap the screen?"

"Don't be ridiculous. I can simply see the massive projectile of your finger hurling itself at me multitudinous times, and I assure you it's quite off-putting."

"I'm sorry," Gabby said, "but you were telling me that

no-face guy was going to kill me. I got a little anxious."

"I said he would *likely* kill you," Edwina clarified, "and only if he's certain you're working with alien life. And of course it won't be him directly. He has leagues of rabid followers and plenty of money to hire someone if he doesn't choose to risk one of them."

"Is that supposed to make me feel better?" Gabby asked shakily. "'Cause not so much."

"Protect yourself. Be on the lookout for anyone unusual. Anyone you don't normally see in the school. Anyone odd or out of place."

As Edwina ticked off the traits, Gabby played back her day in her head. Everyone had been the same as always. Same students, same administrators, same teachers . . .

Not the same teachers.

"Mr. Lau!" Gabby burst. "We had a substitute teacher in math. And he was weird. Really weird. And . . . he threw Wutt on the ground and pounded her with textbooks!"

Edwina raised a single brow. "And you allowed him to do this before you knew it wouldn't harm the girl?"

"It's complicated." Gabby's breath came in short gasps, and she paced as she put the pieces together. "It's got to be him, though. He's the one. He figured it out. He knows Wutt's an alien, he knew she was the book, and he was trying to kill her!"

"It's a possibility," Edwina admitted. For the first time, Gabby saw worry on the old woman's face. "If so, he might think the job is done, which is good. Just be careful. Keep away from this Lau. And keep Wutt out of book form, if that's what he suspects she is. As for your own safety, Houghton wouldn't dare have his people harm a human unless he knew beyond a shadow of a doubt that person was actively involved with alien life. As long as anything his other people see is within the realm of normal explanation, you should be fine."

"His . . . other people?" Gabby asked.

"There may well be others. Houghton often likes to tackle a problem from multiple angles. You'll need to be very careful."

"Wuuuuuttt!!!" the girl cried playfully. Gabby looked over to see Wutt had taken several of Gabby's books out of the knapsack and arranged them like stepping-stones. She giggled as she leaped from one to the other, her mass of red curls flying in the breeze with each jump. Gabby laughed out loud. Wutt was adorable, and all Gabby wanted was to spend the day with her and keep her happy and safe, but after what Edwina had just said . . .

"Are you sure I should still sit for her?" Gabby asked, lowering her voice so Wutt couldn't hear. "I mean, if Houghton thinks I work for you, then maybe Wutt shouldn't be around me. Maybe I shouldn't be the Sitter for the Unsittables."

Edwina's entire face seemed to soften. Even the bun in her hair looked looser. "The very fact that you said that makes you the perfect Sitter for the Unsittables, Gabby."

"But—"

"For as long as aliens have lived among us, there have been frightened, misguided people who would stop at nothing to get rid of them. When we give in to those people, we hand them power. Better to continue doing what we know is right. Show vigilance and caution, of course, but remain steadfast. Do you agree?"

Gabby thought about it. It was the kind of statement she thought her father might have made. The kind of thing she saw in the letters he sent home to Alice when he was overseas. Maybe Gabby had a little of her dad's spirit in her. She sat taller on the piano bench. "I do."

"Good," Edwina said. "Then go about your day. I know how to find you if I need you."

"Wait!" Gabby interjected. "What about if I need *you*?"

But the screen was blank. Gabby shook her phone and the picture returned, but it was just her regular home screen. Edwina was gone. Gabby scrolled across the icons—was there one there for A.L.I.E.N.? Had Edwina installed an app that gave her access to Gabby's phone?

If she had, Gabby didn't see it.

She was on her own.

And her math teacher wanted to kill her—literally.

"We won't let anyone scare us, Wutt," Gabby said. "We'll just be super-careful. Right?"

Wutt had moved Gabby's textbooks. Instead of stepping-stones, they were now piled in a tower, and Wutt wobbled on top of them.

Then she fell.

So much for being super-careful.

Gabby lunged and caught Wutt before the girl hit the floor. Then she checked her watch. "Ten minutes till next period. We should probably head upstairs."

"Wutt," the girl grunted. She strained one arm toward a high spot on the wall and her nostril slits pulsed open and shut as she struggled. Whatever she wanted, she wanted it badly. Gabby looked.

"Oh, that?" Gabby asked. "That's a poster. It shows all the instruments in an orchestra. See? This is a piano. Like this one."

She carried Wutt to the piano, set the girl on top of it, and plinked out the only keyboard tune she knew: "Chop-sticks."

Wutt loved it. She begged for more: "Wutt! Wutt!"

Gabby laughed and played it again. This time Wutt got to her feet and danced.

"Wutt!" she urged when Gabby finished. "Wutt-wutt-wutt!"

"That's the only piano song I know," Gabby said. "I should have brought my French horn. Then I could play you all kinds of things. And I wouldn't have missed my last chance to rehearse before orchestra period today. That's when Maestro Jenkins will make Madison and me play one last time to try and get the solo."

Wutt tilted her head, confused.

"Don't worry about it," Gabby said. "Rehearsal is good, but it's way more important to be here with you and do stuff that makes you happy."

"Wutt! Wutt! Wutt!" Wutt begged. She leaned down and her red curls cascaded over the piano keys as she tried to plink them out on her own. Then she lifted her head, and Gabby swore her eyes were bigger than ever. "Wuuuuuuutt?" she pleaded.

"I would, I really would, but I only play the French horn," Gabby insisted. "I'll show you." She walked back to the poster and pointed. "That's a French horn. And no matter what any tootley-toot flautist or string-loving violinist says, it's the best instrument in the whole orchestra. I remember when I first started playing—"

A loud *thunk* interrupted Gabby's thoughts and she froze. Was it Mr. Lau? Had he found them?

"Wutt?" she asked with a trembling voice. "Did you hear that?"

Wutt didn't answer. Gabby silently darted to the door and peered out the window, but no one was there.

Another loud *thunk*.

Gabby wheeled around. Wutt wasn't on top of the piano anymore.

In fact, Wutt wasn't anywhere in the room.

A French horn, however, was on the floor next to the piano. A French horn that hadn't been there before.

Like all French horns, this one was shaped like a wheel ... but a wheel with a giant megaphone of a horn—the "bell"—bursting out one end, and a mouthpiece sticking out the other.

Unlike most French horns, this one was standing vertically, and *thunk-thunk-thunk*ing up and down.

Gabby beamed. "That's perfect, Wutt! That's exactly what a French horn looks like!"

Thunk. The horn jumped again, edging closer to Gabby.

"Yeah, I see you," Gabby said. "You're an amazing French horn."

THUNK! The horn jumped up and slammed against Gabby's legs.

"Ow! Are you trying to tell me something?"

Gabby picked up the horn and looked it square in the bell.

"I'm not sure what you're trying to say, but—"

In an instant, the horn flipped in Gabby's hands and the mouthpiece plooked into her mouth.

Gabby sputtered. "Hey! You don't actually *swallow* the mouthpiece!"

Twid-twid-twid-twid-twid. The horn's valves moved quickly up and down as if someone were pressing them, and the mouthpiece nudged back against Gabby's mouth.

"I'm getting the sense you want me to play for you," Gabby said.

SCRAAAAWNK!!!

Gabby winced away from the hideous squeak Wutt had forced out of the bell. "Okay," she acquiesced. "I'll do it. I just . . . I mean . . . I'll give it a try."

Gabby slid her right hand into the bell of the horn and tried very hard not to think about what orifice this might be on Wutt. She pressed her lips against the mouthpiece and placed her fingers in position on the valves. She hesitated before starting. She'd taken up the French horn in second grade and hadn't played an instrument that wasn't her own in years. This one felt different; a little lighter, with a slightly different balance.

Plus, it was actually a live alien child.

Yet all that faded when she began to play. The notes of the concerto flowed easily, and she instinctively shifted her hand in and out of the bell to muffle or accentuate just the right moments along the way. Gabby had imagined that Wutt would try playing the song *with* her—that she would move her own valves or shift along Gabby's right arm, with a result that was more playful than melodic, a goofy version of her solo co-performed by an eager but untrained partner.

Instead, Wutt *accentuated* the solo. She didn't manipulate the horn in any way, and yet Gabby could feel how much the little girl loved the music. The horn seemed to vibrate with added emotion, and Wutt's own voice seemed to ring in Gabby's ears, humming in perfect unison with the song. Honestly, it seemed to Gabby that on Wutt, she gave the best performance of her life.

Three minutes later, the last note lingered in the practice room. Wutt transformed back to herself and sat in Gabby's cupped hands. Wutt's liquidy black eyes were wider than ever, and Gabby knew the wonder there shone in her own face as well.

"Thank you, Wutt," Gabby said. "That was beautiful."

Wutt opened her mouth to speak, but all that came out was a hooting sound, like a train whistle blowing. Wutt seemed shocked, and clamped her hands over her belly.

Gabby giggled. "Is that how your stomach growls? Are you hungry?"

Wutt nodded dramatically and filled her eyes with infinite sadness. Gabby laughed out loud. "You don't have to give me the pitiful look. I promise I'll feed you. I have lunch this period. The question is . . . how do I get the food to you? You can't eat if you're a pillow or a French horn, and I can't let anyone see you the way you really are. *Especially* when Mr. Lau's out there."

Wutt wriggled to go down. When Gabby placed her on the floor, she crawled into Gabby's purple knapsack. She stuck out a blue hand and waved. "Wutt!"

"That's good for lunch," Gabby mused. "I'll just keep the knapsack next to me and slip you food. But getting there will be tough. I don't feel right about zipping you in, but we'll see so many people on the way . . ." Gabby thought a minute. "What if you turn into something I can carry? Something normal and inconspicuous."

Wutt leaped into the air, turned into the math book, and slammed herself onto the floor.

"Definitely not that." Gabby shuddered. "What else?"

Wutt quickly morphed into the small black throw pillow she'd been when Gabby met her in the limousine.

"Too weird," Gabby said. "Why would I carry a pillow around?"

The room seemed to shrink, and Gabby backed all the way to the wall as Wutt expanded into a baby grand piano.

"Seriously?" Gabby asked.

The piano's highest notes tinkled in what could only be a laugh.

"Come on, we're already late," Gabby said. "I need something easy. Something it makes sense for me to have out." She nibbled the end of one of her curls as she thought. "Oh! You can be a hat! Maybe a beret, so I can look artsy."

Wutt seemed to understand. As the piano shrunk down, Gabby continued to offer suggestions.

"Or a bowler hat! You know those? Like Charlie Chaplin wore. Really cool. To me, at least. Oh! What about a baseball cap? Zee wears those sometimes and they look really good on her. She doesn't have poufy hair like mine, but maybe it would still—"

Gabby realized the piano had stopped shrinking. It was now a two-foot high furry hot-pink monstrosity of a fuzz bomb, with strands that poked out in all directions as if it had just survived a botched electrocution.

It *was* a hat . . . but it was nothing Gabby would put on her head in a zillion years, and it certainly didn't qualify as inconspicuous.

However, it was bouncing up and down, and Gabby got the sense that it was deliriously pleased with itself. Gabby picked it up and held it so she could look it in what she liked to imagine was the eye.

"It's perfect," Gabby said. She put the hat on, then loaded her things back into her purple knapsack and took off for lunch.

chapter
NINE

For the first time ever, the cafeteria looked to Gabby like a den of potential enemies. She stood in the doorway for a moment, overwhelmed by the sheer number of people inside. Any one of them—several, even— could be working for Houghton. Gabby might right now be looking at someone determined to find her and Wutt and destroy them both.

Her best bet was to act natural and attract as little attention as possible.

"Ew!" Madison Murray screamed. "What is that *thing* on your head?"

The entire cafeteria turned to stare. How could they not? Madison had actually jumped out of her chair, sending it plowing into poor Ellerbee who'd been sweeping the aisle behind her, and her voice was almost shrill enough to crack the windows.

If Gabby couldn't have anonymity, at least she could go for quiet dignity.

"Don't you know?" she calmly asked Madison. "This hat is the latest. My mom catered a lunch for *Trend* magazine, and this was in the gift bag. I'm lucky to have it."

Gabby held her head high as she walked to the cafeteria line. Most people stopped staring, though some glanced at her with newly respectful eyes. Even Ellerbee seemed impressed by Gabby's brush with high fashion. He eyed her hat as she passed.

Madison wasn't as impressed. She huffed something to her friends about top styles never looking right on certain people, but Gabby barely noticed. She concentrated on keeping her head steady, so Wutt wouldn't fall off as she grabbed her tray and checked out the entrée of the day. It was turkey tacos, with chocolate pudding for dessert. Normally, the combo was one of Gabby's favorites, but today she wasn't sure. She looked around to make sure Mr. Lau wasn't anywhere within earshot, then gently cleared her throat. "Excuse me," she asked one of the lunch ladies, "is that gloogen-free?"

The lunch lady stopped assembling tacos and leaned her girth over the counter. "*Gluten*-free?"

"Um . . . no." Gabby again cast her eyes left and right. "*Gloogen.*"

"I don't know what you're talking about, kid."

From farther back in the cafeteria, the doughy form of Chef Ernie looked up from stirring a large vat of tortilla soup. "Gloogen-free?" he asked. "'Course it's gloogen-free."

But he chuckled under his breath as he turned back to the soup. And did he just whip his tongue out to lick his own eye? Gabby thought he did.

"That's okay," she told the lunch lady. "I'll just have peanut butter and jelly. Two please." That choice was always available for kids who didn't like the hot food, and since Ernie had no hand in the sandwiches, Gabby thought it was a safer bet. Once they were on her tray she grabbed two apples, then left the kitchen area to head toward Satchel and Zee, already at their regular table.

Gabby froze in her tracks as she realized her friends weren't alone. Mr. Lau was kneeling between them. Gabby ducked back into the kitchen and watched. They looked like they were deep in conversation.

"This isn't good," Gabby whispered up to her hat. Then she quickly looked around to make sure no one had noticed her talking to her headwear. It didn't seem like anyone had.

Gabby watched as Satchel, Zee, and Mr. Lau laughed like old friends. Then, with a flourish of his cape, Mr. Lau rose and strode away from the table. Gabby waited until he was sitting someplace far away before she joined her friends at their table.

"You just missed Mr. Lau," Zee said. "He's weird, but he's a really nice guy."

Gabby snorted.

"He *is*," Zee said. "He was all concerned after what happened in math class. He asked about you. He wanted to make sure you were okay."

Gabby snorted again.

"Do you need a Kleenex?" Satchel asked. "I have lots. Lots of napkins, at least. Gotta protect the orchestra dress from Aunt Toni's special preconcert meal." Satchel's dress clothes were covered by a mountain of paper napkins. They were tucked into his collar, sleeves, belt, and even between the buttons of his shirt.

"I'm good," Gabby said.

"You might want some napkins anyway," Satchel said. "Aunt Toni said I should share with you. She thinks her food will bring you luck for getting the solo. Dig in."

Satchel indicated the huge spread of food in front of him. His aunt Toni always made lunches for him and his five cousins out of extra food from the family restaurant. Today he had a giant platter of penne with meat sauce, an antipasto salad, and several thick pieces of garlic bread.

"No thanks," Gabby said. She felt a shiver on her head as her hat rocked from side to side. Wutt was hungry. Gabby quickly removed the hat and tucked it into her knapsack, which she left unzipped on the floor next to her seat. Then she slipped one of the sandwiches off her plate and reached it inside. Wutt had clearly already changed back from hat form, because her tiny hands grabbed the sandwich eagerly.

"Ew! Gabby Duran, did you just drop an entire sandwich into your backpack?" Madison Murray screeched from the next row of tables. She was far enough away that she never in a million years should have noticed what Gabby was doing, but of course Madison noticed everything. Her high squeal got someone else's attention, too: Mr. Lau whirled around in his seat, his eyes laser-beaming for Gabby.

"Guess your mom's catering isn't so great if you have to sneak decent food home," Madison snickered. "The *Trend* magazine people probably gave her that hat as a joke."

Madison's friends all giggled appreciatively. Zee whipped around so quickly her braids took a moment to catch up.

"Hey, Madison," she asked, "what's it like to sit at a table so boring you have to spy on other people to make conversation?"

Madison opened her mouth to retort, but Zee shook her head. "Not interested. Over here talking to my friends. Minding our own business. You should try it sometime." She turned back to Gabby and leaned close, so Madison couldn't eavesdrop. "So the math book thing—you gonna tell me what it's all about?"

Gabby wasn't sure she could lie to Zee anymore, especially when Zee just defended her like that. Instead she changed the subject. "Mmmm, Satch, that garlic bread smells really good. Can I have a piece?"

"You'll love it," Satchel said, "but you have to try it with the spread. I know it looks like ectoplasm and smells like bug guts, but I swear it's really good." He opened a small plastic container to reveal a toxic-smelling fluorescent green mush, which he smeared onto the bread. Gabby almost turned it away, but then she knew she'd be back to the conversation about her math book. She held her breath and took a huge bite.

The spread was incredible.

"Wow! This is really great!"

"I know, right? Aunt Toni's new recipe."

From her knapsack, Gabby heard sniffs, then a high-pitched yelping sound, like a puppy begging for a treat.

"What's that noise?" Zee asked.

"What noise?" Gabby asked. She gently nudged her bag

with her foot, but the noise didn't stop.

"Oh snap, I hear it, too," Satchel said.

While her friends looked around for the source of the noise, Gabby quickly slipped the rest of her mush-spread bread into her knapsack. The whines stopped, replaced by a delighted *mmmmm* sound, so low Gabby was sure Zee and Satchel wouldn't hear.

"Whoa, you already finished the bread!" Satchel said when he looked back at Gabby. "Cool, then I can tell you. You know the spread? It sounds totally gross, so I didn't want to say till you ate it, but you know what it is? *Broccolini pesto.*"

"WHAT?!" Gabby exploded. Then she quickly clamped her hand around the top of her knapsack, so Wutt wouldn't jump out to her name.

"I know, right?" Satchel beamed.

Edwina's words from earlier echoed in Gabby's ears. *Don't let her anywhere near broccolini,* she had said. *Hy-per.*

"Do you have any idea how much vitamin J is in broccolini?" Gabby wailed.

"Vitamins run A-B-C-D-E and K," Zee pointed out. "There is no vitamin J."

"I have to go," Gabby said, pushing back from the table. "I have to . . . I have to practice." She pulled up her knapsack from the clenched top, but it was shaking back and forth so hard that she could only lift it an inch before it wrested itself

out of her grip and clunked to the floor. Gabby dropped to her knees next to it and fought to grab the zipper.

"Gabby?" Zee asked. "What's going on?"

"Nothing! What makes you think anything's going on?"

She asked this as she knelt on the floor, outright wrestling with her knapsack, which was now shaking even more violently and had started emitting a sirenlike wail.

The zipper thing wasn't going to happen. Gabby grabbed the knapsack around the middle and scooped it up. She ran to scoot it out of the cafeteria as fast as possible, but she only took two steps before the wail reached a high crescendo and the whole cafeteria turned to stare at Gabby holding her struggling bag.

Then the wailing stopped. The bag went still. And in that second of absolute silence, Gabby thought everything would be okay.

Then a two-foot-tall fuzzy hot-pink hat shot out the top of the bag and landed in the middle of one of the lunch tables.

The good news: Wutt had been clever enough to change out of her regular form. Gabby could apologize to the startled diners and come up with a plausible reason for why her hat might have shot out of her bag.

The bad news: in complete disregard for the way a hat was supposed to act, Wutt bounded up to a hanging light fixture, draped herself over it, swung the fixture back and forth until she gained enough momentum, then sailed across the room and landed on the head of Principal Tate.

The impeccably coiffed principal screamed like a soprano. He jumped to his feet and shrieked, "Get it off! Get it off! Get it off!"

Mr. Lau leaped from his own chair to grab the hat. Gabby's heart nearly stopped as he lunged for it, but Wutt was already on the move. She hopped from head to head around the room. Soon the entire cafeteria was on its feet to watch. A bunch of kids cheered like Wutt was part of the coolest prank ever. Others couldn't figure out *what* she was, and screamed and ducked away any time the wild pink fuzziness got near them.

In the midst of all the chaos, Mr. Lau raced through the aisles, his cape flowing behind him. He vaulted onto some tables, then threw himself onto his belly to slide under others. He lunged for the hat again and again, and would have caught it if Gabby hadn't fought to keep him away. Every time he got close to Wutt, Gabby threw a chair, a tray of food, or in one case another student into his path.

Unfortunately, Mr. Lau wasn't the only danger. Ellerbee was chasing the hat with his broom, swatting at it like it was the world's largest fly. Gabby knew that even a direct hit wouldn't hurt Wutt, but it *could* send her careening toward Mr. Lau, or anyone else who wanted to trap her.

"Ellerbee, no!" Gabby cried. "Don't hit her! I mean . . . *it*! Don't hit *it*!"

Ellerbee didn't listen. He smashed Wutt in the side, and the fuzzy pink hat careened toward the one person in the room paying no attention to the chaos. Madison Murray considered herself far above any drama started by Gabby Duran and sat pointedly eating her chocolate pudding as if nothing in the world were amiss. This is why she was particularly shocked when out of nowhere, a hot-pink furry mass landed square on her pudding bowl, slingshotting the contents into her face and all over her white concert-dress blouse.

"GABBY DURAN!" she screamed as she jumped to her feet. Milk chocolate goodness dripped down her bangs.

"I didn't do it!" Gabby shouted.

Seeing Madison coated in dessert inspired someone in the crowd. "Food fight!" he hollered, and immediately the air was filled with soaring tacos, sandwiches, and flying arcs of chocolate pudding.

"Stop this at once!" Principal Tate tried to boom, but "booming" wasn't really his forte even when things were calm. As Gabby ran past, she saw him standing on his chair and screaming as loud as he could, but she doubted anyone else even knew he was there. Gabby's only concern was Wutt, who was zipping down one of the aisles, zigzagging around table legs, sliding along the food-slippery floor, and bouncing off shocked students' and teachers' heads, legs, and torsos. Gabby raced toward the alien girl, sure this time she'd catch her . . .

. . . when Mr. Lau stepped into the other end of the aisle. His bulk seemed to fill the space, and as Wutt bounced ever closer to him, he whipped off his cape and held it out like a matador, ready to snatch the hat inside.

"Here, hatty hatty! Here, hatty!"

The voice was Satchel's, and as he called out he pulled something into Wutt's path that Gabby knew the girl couldn't resist: a tablecloth on which he'd arranged a giant tower of Aunt Toni's garlic bread, each slice spread thick with broccolini topping.

Gabby knew he was trying to help, but he'd made things even worse. Gabby's heart thudded with wild panic as she imagined Wutt turning back into her regular form in front of everyone to eat the food. "NOOOOO!" she cried.

Gabby lunged for the hat.

Mr. Lau lunged for the hat.

The hat lunged for the tablecloth. The second it landed on the pile of bread, the tablecloth folded itself together and snapped shut to make a small, closed sack around the hat.

At the exact same time, the fire bell rang.

If there was one thing everyone at Brensville Middle School instinctively knew, it was what to do when they heard that sound. Within moments the entire room had emptied as the whole student body and faculty moved outside.

Almost the whole student body and faculty.

Satchel lifted the closed, wiggling tablecloth sack and handed it to Gabby. "I got the idea from *Bloodsucker's Revenge*," he said. "Remember the way they trapped the bloodsucker at the end? Zee rigged this out of some stuff in her pockets and a trigger mechanism from a mousetrap I found in the kitchen . . . which makes me really glad I bring lunch from home."

Gabby took the bag gratefully. "Thanks, Satch."

"Yes, thank you, Satchel," Principal Tate said, grabbing the bag from Gabby. "*I'll* take this. And I very much look forward to hearing your explanation for what just happened here."

chapter
TEN

*g*abby stared at the principal in stunned silence. She opened her mouth as if to speak, then realized she had no possible words, which meant it was just hanging there, open and probably looking quite ridiculous.

"You're not the only one looking forward to an explanation," Ellerbee blared in his Scottish accent. He was red-faced to the top of his white-fringed head as he stormed over to Gabby, Satchel, and Principal Tate. "Who do you think has to clean up this ghastly mess? Starting with this . . . *thing*?!"

Ellerbee grabbed the makeshift bag out of Principal Tate's hand so roughly Gabby's heart fluttered. She hoped

Wutt had turned back into some kind of object so she wouldn't get too battered.

"You don't have to," Gabby said. "I'll take care of that. And the room, too."

She reached for the bag, but Ellerbee pulled it up and away. "Aye, like fun you will, Gabby MacGregor," he growled. "You'll have to get back to *school* and your precious *classes*." He spat the words like they were medieval tortures. "I'm the one stuck *holding the bag,* so I may as well get started."

"You have enough to do with this disaster zone of a cafeteria, I'm afraid, Mr. Ellerbee," boomed a dramatic voice. Gabby's chest crumbled. She knew that rich baritone. She squeezed her eyes shut, wishing she were wrong, but when she opened them, Mr. Lau was right there, adjusting his cape. "It would be my pleasure to relieve you of this one distasteful duty. It's not much, I know, but it's the least I can do."

Apparently, you didn't have to be a friend of A.L.I.E.N. to dislike Mr. Lau, because Ellerbee flinched away as the round, caped man reached for the bag. It gave Gabby just enough time to jump between them.

"Wait!" she cried. "I have to tell you something!"

All eyes spun to Gabby . . . but she had no idea what to say. She'd only spoken up to buy time and keep Wutt out of Mr. Lau's hands.

"Well, Gabby?" Principal Tate snipped impatiently.

"It's okay," Zee said. "You don't have to cover for me."

Gabby whipped her head around. Zee was here?

Ellerbee, Mr. Lau, and Principal Tate looked just as surprised. Only Satchel seemed to know Zee was in the room. She was in a corner, still standing on the chair she'd used to reach the fire alarm. Her braids bounced as she hopped down and made her way to the group.

"The pink thing is mine," she declared. She gave a meaningful look to Ellerbee and added, "It's a robot. For the national robotics championships."

Ellerbee knew all about the national robotics championships. He and Zee talked about them almost every day. So when Zee reached out to him for the sack, Gabby expected him to hand it right over.

He didn't, though. He pursed his lips and held the sack close. He must have been even angrier about the mess than Gabby thought. She was ready to throw herself on the floor, fake some kind of attack, and hope that Zee or Satchel would use the moment to grab the bag, but then Ellerbee sighed and handed the tablecloth sack to Zee.

"Great!" Gabby said brightly. "So now Zee can put the robot back in her locker, and we'll help clean up this mess."

"Not yet," said Principal Tate. He snatched the bag out of Zee's hands and pried open the metal fastener latched around its top. Both Ellerbee and Lau leaned close to peek inside. Gabby nearly swallowed her heart as she chanted over and over again in her head to Wutt, *Be the hat, and be still . . . Be the hat, and be still . . .*

Gabby didn't know if Wutt had actually heard her thoughts, but when Gabby peered into the bag with the others, she saw exactly what she'd hoped to see: a completely normal-looking bright pink fuzzy hat.

"Amazing," Principal Tate mused. "It was so lifelike before."

"That's what I was going for," Zee said. "The bot needs work, though. It wasn't supposed to go crazy like that. So if I could just have it back . . ."

Principal Tate gripped the bag shut. "You know I run a robotics team here at the school," he told Zee for the millionth time. "Why haven't you shared this with us? If you're hoping to win the national robotics championships, why not do it with your school?"

"I prefer to do my own thing, sir."

"And *I* prefer suspending students who irresponsibly release wild machinery into the school population. Should such a student also be responsible for vandalizing school property and triggering a fraudulent fire drill . . . well, that's the kind of student I might have to expel."

Zee paled. "You're going to expel me?"

"Not necessarily," Principal Tate offered.

"I don't understand," Zee said.

But Gabby did. And from the worried murmur of "Oh snap" next to her, she knew Satchel did, too.

"You need a reprieve from your punishment, and I need success for my robotics team. So I'll hold on to this"—Principal Tate held up the tablecloth sack—"and you'll join me and the team after school, when you can disassemble the robot for us and show us how it's made."

"NO!" Gabby screamed so loudly everyone jumped—including the hat in the bag. Luckily, they were all too stunned to notice.

"I mean," she clarified, "Zee's watching my and Satchel's concert after school. She can't go to robotics."

"You'll play many more concerts," Principal Tate clucked. "She can miss today's. Now all three of you, get to class. Mr. Ellerbee can handle this mess on his own."

Gabby could have sworn Ellerbee actually growled at this, but Principal Tate didn't notice. He turned on his heel and strode toward the cafeteria doors, Wutt's sack gripped tightly in his fist. Mr. Lau scurried behind him, his cape flapping in his wake.

"You know, Principal Tate," Mr. Lau said, "I have quite a history with robotics myself, and I've heard marvelous things about your helmsmanship of the team. If it's not too much trouble, I'd very much like to join you this afternoon for the disassembly. It would be a true revelation to see just how that thing ticks. And to watch you in action, of course."

The thought of Wutt being "disassembled" had Gabby in such shock she froze. She could only stare in horror as Principal Tate and Mr. Lau walked out of the cafeteria in lockstep, heads bent close like gossiping middle school girls.

Then she snapped back to life.

"Wait!" she wailed, and scurried after them. She pushed through the cafeteria doors, but Principal Tate and Mr. Lau had already turned the corner and were far away. Worse, lunch period had officially ended, and the hall between Gabby and the two men was filled with students. As Gabby darted her way through the sea of people, Satchel and Zee caught up with her.

"You want to tell us what's really in that bag?" Zee asked as they people-dodged.

"Desperately," Gabby said, "but I—"

"Gabby Duran!" screeched Madison Murray. She stepped in front of Gabby and planted herself like a brick wall. Madison's eyes glowered so ferociously Gabby was afraid hot lava would spew out of them and melt her to ash. Madison's wet, stringy bangs flopped in her face as she screamed, "You did this on purpose!"

"I didn't!" Gabby insisted. She tried to sidestep Madison, but the girl moved with her. Madison tugged at the grotesque blotch of faded brown on her once-white silk-and-lace blouse. It gave off a dizzying mix of soap and chocolate smells that churned Gabby's stomach.

"You thought if you ruined my clothes," Madison sneered, "I couldn't do the concert and the solo. But guess what—my mom's bringing me a new blouse. You failed. I will get that solo, Gabby. I'll play better than you, and even in my second-best top, I'll look better than you, too."

"You always look better than me, Madison," Gabby said. "I'm really sorry, but I have to go." She feinted to the left, then when Madison mirrored her, ducked to the right and ran.

"I'm not going to run in heels, Gabby!" Madison shouted. "But believe me, this is *so* not over!"

Gabby didn't doubt it, but she was far more concerned about Wutt. She thundered down the hall. It had emptied out almost completely now that the next class period had begun. Even Satchel and Zee had disappeared to class.

Mr. Lau and Principal Tate were nowhere to be seen.

Unless . . .

Gabby walked slowly toward Principal Tate's office. She moved carefully, so her shoes wouldn't slap against the floor and alert any teachers to her loitering during class time. She crouched low against the bottom of Principal Tate's door, then slowly slid upward, so she could peer into the window. . . .

"Gabby!"

It was Zee's whisper-hissed voice, but it surprised Gabby so much she screamed.

"What was that?" rang out Principal Tate's voice, and from his office Gabby heard a chair anxiously scraping along the floor.

Principal Tate was getting up. He was going to come out and catch Gabby and send her back to class before she could help Wutt!

But then hands grabbed her from behind and Zee's voice hissed, *"Come on!"*

Zee pulled Gabby across the hall into Ellerbee's office and slammed the door just as they heard Principal Tate fling open his own door and stomp into the hall.

"Why'd you scream?" Zee whispered.

"You scared me!" Gabby whispered back.

"I told you we should have clamped a hand over her mouth before we said anything," Satchel added. He was in the tiny office too. "It's what they do in the movies."

"Shhh!" Zee hushed him. She pulled Gabby down next to her and they huddled on the floor. Ellerbee's door had never fit well—an injustice he didn't feel like he should have to fix himself—so there was a wide space at the bottom between the sill and the door. Gabby crouched there with Zee and peered out at Principal Tate's pinstriped knees, which were joined a moment later by a pair of large black ballooning trousers and the billow of a cape.

"I'm sure it was nothing," Mr. Lau said. "My opinion, you're on edge from all the hullabaloo. Please let me take the robot off your hands. One less thing to trouble you during the day, and I'll bring it back for your robotics meeting."

"No," Gabby whispered. "No-no-no-no-no-no . . ."

"No," Principal Tate echoed. "It's no trouble. The robot's fine where it is. But please, Eumeris, do come check out the disassembly. I'll be interested to get your opinion."

The black-trousered knees seemed to shift back and forth, hesitating, then Mr. Lau said, "I look forward to it. I shall see you then!"

Gabby and Zee watched Mr. Lau's bottom third stride down the hall, then saw Principal Tate's legs return to his office. The door clicked shut.

"Eumeris?" Satchel gawped.

"What did he mean 'the robot is fine where it is'?" Gabby worried. "Where *is* it?"

"Locked in his filing cabinet," Zee said. "Satch and I followed them down and checked it out through the window. Satchel can show you."

"Seriously?" Satchel asked. "We're just going to zoom right over the fact that the guy's name is Eumeris?"

"Satchel!" Gabby urged.

"Fine." He pulled out his cell phone, swiped to video, and handed it to Gabby. "We used my super-spy tactics. We pretended to take a selfie in front of Principal Tate's door but actually shot a video. Check it out."

Gabby pressed Play. She couldn't hear anything over the dull roar of the crowded school hallway, and the foreground of the shot was Zee and Satchel's foreheads as they posed for their staged close-up, but behind them Gabby could see Principal Tate's entire office through his window. Mr. Lau was chatting away saying who-knew-what and reached out to take the bag with Wutt in it, but Principal Tate shook his head. He opened the bottom drawer of his filing cabinet, plopped the still-closed bag inside, then pulled a set of keys from his pocket and locked the drawer again as the video ended.

"I have to get her out of there," Gabby said as she handed the phone back to Satchel.

"I get it," Zee said. "And we've totally got your back. Just maybe you could tell us what 'she' is first."

Gabby looked at Satchel, his brown eyes wide with nervous interest. She looked at Zee, her blond braids cocked to one side as her fixed blue-eyed gaze tried to peer into Gabby's head and dig out the facts for herself. If it weren't for the two of them, Wutt could be in even worse shape than she was now. Plus, they'd sacrificed to help her. Already Zee had risked expulsion and agreed to suffer the tortures of Principal Tate's Robotics class, and they were both in the middle of skipping their sixth period classes. Edwina wouldn't approve, but Gabby owed them the truth.

"I'll tell you," she said, "but you have to swear-swear-swear you won't breathe a word to anyone. Ever. *Ever*. It's that huge."

"Sworn," Zee said.

"I'm out," Satchel said.

Zee wheeled on him. "You're what?"

"I'm in for the helping!" Satchel clarified. "I'm just *really* bad at keeping secrets. I don't want to be the guy who messes up and lets everything out."

"Yeah, but I want to know," Zee insisted, "and we're all in a little room."

Satchel scrunched his face, then lit up with an idea. "Oh snap!" He turned his back to the wall, put his hands over his ears, and hummed. Zee just stared at him.

"I want to make fun of him," she finally told Gabby, "but it'll work. The sound waves he's creating will help counteract ours. Like noise-canceling headphones."

Then Zee folded her arms and raised an eyebrow—Gabby's cue to start talking. Gabby twisted the end of a curl in her mouth, frowned, then blurted out the insanity as fast as she could.

"The-hat-is-a-little-girl-named-Wutt-and-she's-an-
alien-from-another-planet-and-I'm-babysitting-her."

"YES!" Zee howled, slapping her palm on Ellerbee's
desk. "I knew it!"

Satchel started humming louder and bouncing his head
from side to side. Apparently, Zee's outburst overcame his
noise-canceling capabilities.

"You knew it?" Gabby asked incredulously. "How could
you know it?"

"Hello—the math thing? Even before your freak-out
over the book, you must have said the word 'alien' like a zillion times. And on Monday when you were all, 'Space aliens?
I didn't bring up space aliens. You were the one who brought
up space aliens.' So what's the deal? What planet is she from?
What galaxy? Milky Way? No, outside Milky Way. Gotta be
an outer galaxy, she probably got here by wormhole. What
kind of galaxy? Spiral? Elliptical? Irregular? Are there other
people from her planet here, too? Oh wow, human-centric
much, Zee? Like she's really a 'person.' Hello, insensitive!
Okay, I'm stopping. Give me the scoop."

Zee stared at Gabby, her eyes eager and dancing. Gabby
just stood there, slack-jawed.

"Um . . . I don't . . . really . . . know?"

"You *what*? You didn't ask about her planet? About her
galaxy? About her *biology*?"

Gabby twirled one of her low-hanging curls around her finger. "I've never been really good at biology. . . ."

"But her biology is incredible!" Zee roared loudly enough that Satchel again had to modulate his humming. "One cell of it could probably change the way we think about *everything*! I mean, she can turn into things, right? Like the hat and the math book . . ."

"Uh-huh. And a pillow. And she was a French horn for a little while. And a piano."

"Are you kidding me? And you never asked how she did it?"

"No," Gabby admitted. "I was thinking more about fun things I could show her. You know, keeping her happy. And safe."

Zee's goggle-eyed dismay froze on her face, then melted into an abashed smile. "You're a way better person than I am, Gabs. You're right. Fun and happy and safe. No skin cells."

"Unless Mr. Lau gets a hold of her," Gabby said. "He's from this organization . . . There's a lot to tell, but he knows what she is, and he wants to get rid of her. And me too, if I get in his way."

"Seriously? Mr. *Lau?*"

"He's dangerous. And so is Principal Tate if he brings her to robotics and tries to take her apart. She might look like an object, but if she's ripped apart or impaled"—the words stuck like cotton in Gabby's throat and she had to choke them out—"it'll be for real."

Zee made a gagging face, then brightened. "I promised Tate I'd go to robotics. I'll make sure she's okay."

Gabby shook her head. "Can't risk it. What if he tries to take her out and mess with her before then? I have to get her out of there and someplace safe, but I can't do it while Principal Tate's in his office."

"Done," Zee said. "Satch and I will get his attention, then you can slip in."

"No," Gabby said. "He's already suspicious of you guys. I don't want you to get in trouble."

"I can set off another fire alarm," Zee offered.

It was possible, but Gabby worried that Zee would get caught. She needed another way to distract Principal Tate, and soon.

"Great piles of haggis!" Ellerbee exclaimed as he opened the door and saw Satchel and the girls. "What are you trying to do to me? First the blunderbuss in the cafeteria, now you hide out in my office to ditch your class and nearly scare my heart clean stopped!"

"Sorry," Gabby said.

"Our bad, L-Man," Zee added. "The caf was a total accident, and we're here because Gab's in a major bind."

"And the boy?" Ellerbee asked, jutting a thumb toward

Satchel. "Looks to me like he's dead lost it."

Gabby and Zee looked. Satchel still faced the wall, held his hands over his ears, and hummed; but now he'd given the hum a tune. He danced to it, sliding back and forth across two feet of space and shaking his booty in a way that made Gabby desperately wish she had time to pull out her cell phone and tape it. This was the kind of serious entertainment value that would only skyrocket over time.

Instead she tapped his shoulder.

"Is it over?" he said as he spun to the girls. "Did I miss the big secret?"

"Big secret, did you say?" Ellerbee mused.

Satchel threw his hands in the air. "You see? Even taking all precautions, this is what happens. I am a hazard to myself and others. I cannot be allowed anywhere near the major plot points of my life."

"Does this secret have to do with Gabby McGregor's 'major bind'?" Ellerbee asked.

Gabby locked eyes with Zee, who shrugged—this was Gabby's call.

"Actually," Gabby said, "it does. It's about the hat."

"The robot?" he asked knowingly.

Zee grimaced. "Yeah, okay. It's not really a robot."

"It's not?" Satchel asked. "Wait, don't tell me. Should I start humming again?"

Zee ignored him and kept talking to Ellerbee. "You gotta trust us on this, L-Man. We can't say what the hat is, but it's majorly important to Gabby and she has to get it away from Tate, like, now."

"Except he's locked in his office, and I don't know how long he'll be there," Gabby added. "If someone could distract him, I think I could get the hat out . . ."

"Someone?" Ellerbee asked archly. "Like a certain custodial worker, aye?"

Gabby reddened. She hated to ask Ellerbee for help. It's not like she was Zee and the two of them were friendly. "Well," she started, "only if it's not a big problem. Zee said she and Satchel could do it, but I don't want to get them in trouble."

"And you're not so worried about ol' Ellerbee, is that it?" he asked. The words stung, but he said them kindly, and he smiled afterward. "Wouldn't have it any other way. But even if you get the mysterious hat out of the office, you'll need a place to keep it safe, aye?"

"I think she's got it covered, L-Man," Zee said.

Gabby knew what she meant. Once Gabby had Wutt in hand, the little girl could turn into almost anything and stay hidden in Gabby's knapsack. That trick hadn't thrown off Mr. Lau, though, and it might not throw off any other members of G.E.T. O.U.T. at the school. If there was a better way to make sure Wutt stayed in one piece, Gabby wanted to know about it.

"Do you have something in mind?" she asked.

"Indeed I do, Gabby MacGregor. Tower classroom 3A."

"Wait," Satchel said. "I thought the Tower was closed off because it was haunted. By the spirit of an eighth grader who failed his finals and hurled himself out the window to his death."

Ellerbee laughed. "Very dramatic, that is, but not a bit of it true. They closed the Tower because it's old and expensive to heat and cool. District's been planning to tear it down for decades now, but that costs money, too. Better to make the custodial staff drag his old bones up there to clean it every week. On the plus side . . ." Ellerbee pulled a large, round key chain from a peg on wall and worked off two keys. He handed them both to Gabby. "Gold one works the door to the Tower itself, silver one's 3A. It's the highest one. Best place for a person to hide out, if hiding out was necessary . . . though you didn't hear it from me."

He gave a deep laugh, and for the first time, Gabby really took in Ellerbee's kind, round face and sparkling eyes. Add in long white hair and a beard and he could be a Scottish Santa Claus. It was all Gabby could do to stop from hugging him. "Thank you, Ellerbee," she gushed. "This is perfect."

Just then the bell rang, which was also perfect because

Satchel and Zee could slip out of Ellerbee's office and blend in with the other students heading to seventh period. They still needed an excuse for ditching sixth, and as Gabby watched them disappear down the hall she heard Satchel suggesting they say they were kidnapped by rogue army mech-bots. Zee countered that helping to clean the cafeteria might be a touch more believable.

As for Gabby, she was now about to skip her second school period ever, but it was worth it to save Wutt. Her plan was to hide out with the alien girl through seventh period. Then she could have Wutt turn into something tiny and slip that into her pocket for the eighth period orchestra final solo-showdown with Madison Murray, as well as for the concert itself. After that she could bring Wutt home, and they could play in Gabby's room until Edwina came to pick her up.

"You ready, Gabby MacGregor?" Ellerbee asked. "I promise I'll keep him busy as long as I can."

Gabby nodded, then stayed in Ellerbee's office and peeked through the space in the jamb while he knocked on Principal Tate's door. "Principal Tate, it's Ellerbee, and I could sorely use your opinion in the cafeteria." Gabby couldn't hear Tate's response, but then Ellerbee spoke up again. "Oh, aye, I believe you'll want to be seeing this. Won't take but a minute."

Gabby held her breath as she waited the endless seconds

until Principal Tate decided whether or not he'd leave his office. Finally, he emerged, his entire face scrunched into a frown. "This had better be important, Ellerbee. I have more meaningful things to do than check up on a custodial job."

"No doubt you do, sir," Ellerbee said as he walked two steps behind Tate down the hall. "No doubt you do."

He shot Gabby an okay sign before they turned the corner, and Gabby counted to five before she hoisted her purple knapsack over her shoulder, darted out of Ellerbee's office, and ran into Principal Tate's. It was unlocked; he only locked it when he left school each day. Gabby's heart thumped in her chest as she closed the door behind her. Now she wasn't just skipping class, she was trespassing in the principal's office. If she were caught . . .

She couldn't think about that. She wouldn't be caught. Not if she moved quickly.

Principal Tate's office was three times the size of Ellerbee's closet, complete with a huge wooden desk that gleamed with polish, a plush leather rolling chair, seats and a couch for visitors, and a majestic bookcase that spanned one full wall. The office felt grand but ancient, as evinced by the globe on its tall mahogany pedestal—the globe that showcased a giant red U.S.S.R.

Gabby only scanned all that. Her attention went immediately to the tall vertical filing cabinet. The one piece of cold metal amidst all the warm wood, it looked chillingly to Gabby like the drawers of a morgue. She crouched down and leaned close to the crack around the bottom drawer.

"Wutt, are you there? It's me, Gabby. I'm alone, so you can talk. Can you hear me?"

Nothing. Nothing at all. Panic sizzled across Gabby's skin.

"Wutt? If you're in there, please answer me!"

The voice that came back sounded tiny and far away. "Wutt?"

"Oh good! I'm so glad you're okay!" Gabby gushed. She looked over her shoulder to make sure she was alone, then spoke in a rush. "We don't have time. Turn into something really, really thin, like a piece of paper or string. You know what those are, right? Paper or string? Then you can fit out of the sack and through the crack around the drawer. Do you understand? Wutt? Do you understand what I'm saying?"

When Wutt didn't respond, Gabby pushed her lips against the crack to say, "Wutt?" again . . . and nearly choked when a paper clip flew into her mouth and hit the back of her throat. She coughed it into her palms, where the paper clip morphed into a tiny girl with blue skin, black oval eyes, slit-nostrils, and an impossibly large mane of red curls.

"WUTT!" she cried, throwing her arms around Gabby's neck.

Gabby hugged her close. "Oh, Wutt, I was so worried." She pulled the little girl back to look her in the eye and said, "Don't ever freak me out like that again, okay?"

"Wutt?"

"I know, I know, I'm the one who let you have the broccolini, totally my fault, just . . ." She pulled Wutt close again. "Stay safe, okay?"

"Wutt," the little girl agreed, and hugged Gabby a little tighter until Gabby pulled her back again.

"I'm glad you're out, but we're still in a lot of trouble. I don't know if you were listening when Edwina told me, but there are some bad people after you, and we *cannot* let them see you looking like yourself, got it?"

Wutt's eyes grew enormous, and she trembled in Gabby's arms as she pointed behind Gabby's shoulder. "Wutt?"

Gabby wheeled around. Mr. Lau was standing in the doorway, a wicked grin stretched across his face. "Oh, I think she's got it," he said.

chapter ELEVEN

"We need to converse, Gabby Duran," Mr. Lau said as he stepped closer, his cape swirling around his body, "but first I must insist you turn over that alien child."

Mr. Lau lunged forward, arms outstretched. Gabby knew she wouldn't stand a chance wrestling Wutt away from him. The only move she could think of went against her every instinct, but she had no choice. She cringed, held her breath, then hurled Wutt at the man's feet, shouting, "Something slippery, Wutt!"

Wutt splooshed onto the floor, a puddle of oil on which

Mr. Lau's feet lost purchase and slid out from under him. As he fell, Wutt quickly turned back into herself and darted away as Mr. Lau's bulky body thudded to the ground. He landed flat on his back, his head thumping loudly against the hard wood.

He didn't move. Alarm prickled the skin under Gabby's arms into a cold sweat. Was he alive? Terrified, she tiptoed slowly to his side and leaned close to look for a pulse in his neck.

"Uuuuuugggghhh," he groaned, breathing a gust of moldy-fish breath straight up Gabby's nose. She recoiled and grabbed Wutt, then tossed the girl into her purple knapsack.

"Something small, Wutt," she said. "I'm going to zip you in and get out of here."

Gabby didn't know what the girl became, but the knapsack had just enough heft when she tossed it over her shoulder that she imagined it was some kind of book or binder. She checked the clock. Seventh period was more than halfway over. She was lucky Ellerbee had kept Principal Tate away as long as he had, but he could be back any second. She leaned out the door to make sure the coast was clear, then barreled down the halls as fast as she could. She turned corners, racing past the stairwell that led down to the music rooms, past the stairs that led to the upper-floor classrooms, all the way down to the far end of the school, and the never-used door that led to the Tower.

Gabby glanced over her shoulder, pulled the gold key from her pocket, unlocked the door, then shut it behind her. The air smelled of must lightly covered by pine cleaner, and though Gabby would have loved to peek in at the post-apocalyptically abandoned classrooms, she instead stormed up the stairs to the top floor, scanned the doors for 3A, then used the silver key to open it. It didn't have a twist or push-button lock on the inside; the key locked it here as well. Gabby eagerly twisted the key in the lock to seal herself safely inside.

The room was large, its carpet streaked with ancient skids and splotches, and divoted by long-gone chairs and desks. It also held fresh vacuum tracks. Clearly, Ellerbee had tried his best, but the damage here was permanent. The walls were faded orange, with a giant rectangle of brighter orange along one, where the blackboard once hung. A row of cracked-paned windows ran along another wall, each one so wide that Gabby understood how the suicide rumor had started. If someone did want to jump, the windows could easily accommodate them. When she peered out, the sidewalk below looked like a child's toy.

This was the kind of room that would have given Satchel nightmare visions of zombie teachers and vampire students, but it was tucked away and locked, and that made it perfect for Gabby. She plopped down in the middle of the floor, shrugged off her knapsack, and opened it.

"Wutt?" the girl asked, popping her red-curled head out of the bag.

"Yeah, we're good," Gabby said.

She winced as an idea crossed her mind, and Wutt noticed. The little girl crawled the rest of the way out of Gabby's knapsack and clambered into her lap. She looked up at Gabby with deep concern in her eyes. "Wutt?"

Gabby smoothed her hand over the girl's curls. "I don't know . . . I just wonder if maybe we should stay here all day. Skip orchestra, skip the concert . . . sneak you out afterward and keep you in my room until Edwina comes to get you."

Wutt cocked her head to one side as if confused, then leaped off Gabby's lap and twirled like a ballerina. Her long nostril-slits vibrated as she hummed the notes to Gabby's solo.

"I know," Gabby agreed. "I don't *want* to miss it, but if it'll keep you safe . . ."

She pulled her phone from her knapsack. She planned to text Satchel and have him tell Maestro Jenkins she was sick and would have to miss the concert, but before she could do it, she heard a key turning in a lock. Gooseflesh chilled Gabby's skin. She shoved her phone in her back pocket, tossed her knapsack on her back, grabbed Wutt into her arms, and backed into a corner. "Change, Wutt," she whispered. "Quickly."

When the door swung open, Gabby was holding her breath . . . and a giant beach ball in her hands.

"Gabby MacGregor?"

"Ellerbee!" Gabby cried with relief. She stepped out of the shadows to see the old man standing in the door. He held a large sack, heavy enough to pull him down on his left side, and breathed heavily from the climb upstairs.

"I should've known it was you," Gabby said. The beach ball in her arms was so wide that Gabby had to struggle to see the janitor around it. "I can't thank you enough for this place. You're the best."

Ellerbee smiled and his shoulders drooped humbly. "Not at the moment I'm not, lassie. But I will be. When you give me the alien child and I get my million-dollar reward."

Gabby felt her stomach curdle. She clutched the beach ball closer. When she spoke, her voice sounded like a frightened squeak. "Wait . . . what?"

"Aye, you know what I'm talking about. Let's not play games. It looks like a pink fuzzy hat, but we both know it's more than that."

Gabby's breath flowed a little easier. At least Ellerbee thought Wutt was still a hat. He didn't know she could change. That could buy her some time to figure a way out of this.

"I don't understand," Gabby said. "I thought Mr. Lau was the one after her."

Ellerbee's furry white brows shot up. "A girl child, is she? Eh, all the same." He bent over to re-lock the door from the inside and seal in Gabby and Wutt. "As for *Mr.* Lau, I saw what he was trying to do. The rich man with the scrambled face on the phone chat told me there'd be others. But I had the inside track, didn't I now? We're friends, you and I. So let's make this easy. Hand me the child, and we can forget this ever happened. Where is she, in your backpack?"

Gabby's mind whizzed with options. She could give him her knapsack and try to run out with the beach ball, but he'd look inside and know she'd tricked him before she could unlock the door. She could throw Wutt at him like she did with Mr. Lau, but Ellerbee was too old to handle a smack on the head. If anything happened to him . . . No matter how crazy he was acting now, Gabby couldn't live with herself if he got hurt because of her.

Gabby placed the beach ball on the floor behind her and moved closer to Ellerbee, trying to reason with him. "Ellerbee, you're a really good man. If you understood what Houghton—the scrambled face guy—if you knew what he'd do to her, I don't think you'd want to hand her over. He'll hurt her. Or worse. And she's an innocent kid."

Ellerbee laughed so hard he started to cough. He doubled over, and Gabby wondered if she should help him or try to sneak past while he struggled for breath. The choice was made for her when he stood tall again and pointed something at her that he'd pulled off his belt.

"Is that a gun?" Gabby gasped.

"Easy there, lassie. Just a stun gun. I don't want to use it, but I will if I have to. As for the girl, I've spent forty years cleaning up after innocent kids and got not a lick of respect, nor a lining of my pockets. If one little alien girl has to have a tough time for me to get my due, I can live with that."

Gabby considered her options. The stun gun could knock her out, but only if Ellerbee touched her with it. Gabby could easily outrun him. If she had to let him chase her around the room until he got tired enough that she had a second to unlock the door and escape, that was fine with her. She crossed her arms and made her face stony. "I'm sorry, Ellerbee. I can't let that happen."

Ellerbee sighed, then pulled two large items from the bag at his side. Gabby recognized them immediately. They were the Shoombas—the two robot vacuum cleaners Zee had rigged with foot clamps and jet power for him. As he slipped his feet into the clips on top of each machine, he said, "I'm sorry, too, Gabby MacGregor, but I'm done cleaning up after other people."

"But . . . aren't those vacuum cleaners?"

"They are, lassie," Ellerbee agreed. "And they're also how I'm going to shut you down and get what I need." He kicked his vacuum-clad heels together, and the twin engines roared to life. Holding the stun gun in front of him, he zoomed toward Gabby. Panic froze her for just a second, which was all it took for Ellerbee to lunge at her with the sizzling mouth of the gun.

"Here!" Gabby shouted. She shrugged off her purple knapsack and hurled it across the room. It landed near the door, and Ellerbee quickly swerved to get it. With his attention on the bag, Gabby ran to the nearest window. Her breath rasped in her throat as she pushed up on the ancient edging to try to open it, and she cried out when it stuck. Grunting with effort, she leaned in and pushed once more. The window flew upward, and Gabby drank in the cold fall breeze.

"It's not in here!" roared Ellerbee, tossing aside the knapsack. His jet engines zoomed to life again, and Gabby knew she had no time. She grabbed the beach ball and shoved it out the window, but it was too big around. It stuck halfway through.

"I've got you now, lassie!" Ellerbee growled right behind her, and as Gabby pushed on the ball with all her might she cried, "Change, Wutt! Change to something smaller!"

Wutt did as she was told. She turned from a giant beach ball to a tennis ball . . . just as Gabby thrust all her weight into a final shove. With nothing to push against, Gabby's momentum spilled her out of the window.

Gabby's stomach climbed into her throat, and she had no idea if she was pointed up or down. She scrambled and clawed for something to hold, but there was nothing. She was falling. If she were lucky, she'd break every bone in her body. If she weren't lucky . . .

Gabby shut her eyes tight. She remembered the tennis ball falling out of the window first. At least Wutt would be okay. If the girl was smart, she'd roll into some tall grass and stay there until Edwina found her.

The wind flapping against her hurt Gabby's ears. She clapped her hands over them and waited for it all to be over. She tried not to imagine the final thump. How much it would hurt. How long she'd lie there until someone called an ambulance. Or what Ellerbee would do if he found her first.

THUMP!

The shock of landing knocked out Gabby's breath . . . but she didn't feel any pain. She lay still, waiting for it to kick in, an agonizing torture so overwhelming she'd beg to lose consciousness.

It didn't happen.

In fact, she felt comfortable. Cozy, even. She rolled onto her stomach and opened her eyes.

She was lying on a five-foot-thick air mattress that had cushioned her fall.

"Wutt?" Gabby cried delightedly.

The little girl gently deflated, easing Gabby to the ground before turning back into her own shape and raising her arms with a ta-da shout, "Wutt-WUTT!"

"You are *amazing*!"

Gabby hugged the alien girl, then a faraway gasp of "Hollerin' haggis!" made her look up.

Ellerbee leaned out of the top Tower classroom window. Even from this distance, Gabby could see his mouth gaped open and his eyes wide. Ellerbee knew Wutt could change now, and he'd seen her in her true form. That was bad. At least he was all the way up in the Tower. By the time he got down here, Gabby would have Wutt far away from the school.

Then twin jets roared, and Gabby watched in horrified awe as Ellerbee lifted first one Shoomba-clad foot and then the other out the Tower window. He stepped out into sheer nothingness, the jet-powered vacuum cleaner robots supporting him as he lowered slowly to the ground. He still wielded the stun gun, and Gabby knew once he landed he could use the jets to outpace them almost instantly.

"We have to get out of here, Wutt," Gabby murmured. "Fast."

She was answered by another engine roar, this one much closer than Ellerbee's. She wheeled around. Where Wutt had been a second ago sat a large motorcycle, the same blue as the girl's skin, with painted flames the color of her fiery curls.

"I don't know how to drive a motorcycle, Wutt!" Gabby yelled.

The motorcycle revved.

"I don't have a helmet!"

The motorcycle scooted forward a few feet.

"I'm only twelve! I don't have a license!"

The next roar was from Ellerbee's Shoombas, and when Gabby spun she could see the sizzle of the stun gun, ready to bite into her skin.

Gabby screamed and climbed onto the motorcycle, which shot away so quickly Gabby was nearly thrown off. She forced herself to lean forward over the handlebars and grip until her knuckles went white. Her curls smacked across her face and blindfolded her eyes. She peeked over her shoulder. Ellerbee was following them on the Shoombas. He wasn't as fast as Wutt, but his teeth gripped in determination as he leaned into the chase and tried to put on speed.

a-*WOO*-ga!

It was the same hideous noise she'd heard earlier in the day, when she was on her way down to the music room. She pulled her phone out of her pocket and pressed the button on the bottom. Edwina's face filled the screen, calm and efficient as always.

"Gabby?" she began.

"Edwina!" Gabby shouted. The wind blew curls into her mouth as she spoke and she spit them away. "I really need your help!"

"Excuse me?" Edwina asked, raising an eyebrow. "I can't hear you. We seem to have a bad connection."

"Can you *see* me?" Gabby wailed as Wutt zoomed them beneath some low-hanging branches that slapped leaves into her face. They were racing through the woods that separated the school from a residential area, and the walking paths weren't made to accommodate motorbikes. "I'm having a little trouble here!"

"Things are going well, you say?" Edwina said. "So glad to hear it. I just wanted to check in with you because there's been a change of plans. I'll be picking up Wutt at your school right after your concert. I'll meet you both in the auditorium."

"No, Edwina, I won't be at the concert!" Gabby said as several bugs smacked against her cheeks. "We're being chased by G.E.T. O.U.T.! I need backup! Come get us now—I need you!"

"Hmm . . . Still crackling in and out, but I assume you understand and we're all settled. I'll see you in a bit, then." The screen clicked to black.

"NO!" Gabby screamed to the now-blank phone. A ball of disappointment swelled in her throat and she thought she might cry. "What are we going to do, Wutt?"

Then Gabby looked up and screamed. They had left the woods and were on a street . . . in the wrong lane . . . with a car zooming right toward them. "Wutt!" Gabby wailed as the car's horn honked. "Look out!"

Wutt swerved to miss the car, but her wheels skidded out from under her, and the motorcycle careened to a steep grassy embankment at the side of the road. Gabby could picture her legs being crushed by the motorbike as it fell on top of her. She winced, but Wutt changed just as they lost balance and toppled. She became a rag doll version of herself and tumbled into Gabby's arms as they rolled down the hill. The ground and the sky kept changing places as Gabby tumbled. When she stopped, she jumped to her feet.

The world was still spinning, but she wasn't hurt. She even knew where they were. She and Wutt had landed not far from a huge sprawling playground—the same one she came to all the time while babysitting. It was full of kids right now, all of them squealing with glee as they scrambled around jumping, swinging, and playing. Gabby recognized a lot of them, and was so happy to see *them* happy she almost forgot the terrible danger she was in . . .

. . . until she heard a twin-jet roar and wheeled around to see Ellerbee, his stun gun poised as his Shoombas zoomed him swiftly down the hill and right toward Wutt and Gabby.

chapter
TWELVE

there was no time to think. Gabby scooped up rag doll Wutt and ran toward the playground.

"Hey!" she called out. "April! Sienna! Jordan! Madeline! Look what I've got!"

Gabby's voice must have sounded as panicky as she felt, because several parents and nannies who sat on benches around the playground turned around, alarmed. Their faces relaxed when they saw Gabby though, and they waved and smiled.

The kids were more exuberant. Most of them had known Gabby since they were infants. "GABBY!" they screamed, and stampeded toward her in a swarm. Gabby knelt down as the squealing kids cascaded over her, hugging every part of her they could reach. Gabby tucked Wutt under one arm and used the other to hug back every kid she could. As she did, she glanced over her shoulder. Ellerbee stood glowering from a group of trees several yards away. He'd removed the Shoombas to look less conspicuous, but he didn't dare come closer. Much as he might want to grab Wutt, a lone man causing a commotion at a kids' playground would only send every mom, dad, and nanny reaching for their phones to dial 911. The longer Gabby could keep Wutt with the throng of kids, the better off she'd be.

"Is that your doll?" a little girl named April asked.

"Yes, she is!" Gabby replied. She pulled Wutt from under her arm and held the rag doll out so she was standing on the ground. As always, Wutt had done an impeccable job of transforming herself. She stood about three feet tall, which was about the same size as most of the kids. Like the real alien, her doll-skin was blue, and she had giant black button eyes, thick red curls of yarn, and a painted-on smile. She wore a red gingham dress, knee socks, and black strappy shoes. Her face was dotted with freckles just like Gabby's.

She was enchantingly adorable. The kids backed away a bit to admire her.

"She looks so soft," a doe-eyed four-year-old named

Bianca cooed. "Can I hug her?"

"You sure can," Gabby said.

Bianca wrapped her arms around Wutt and squeezed her tight. Wutt tried to hug her back, and Gabby had to move fast to make it look like she was the one moving the doll's arms around Bianca's body.

"I love her!" Bianca said. "What's her name?"

"It's Wu—"

Gabby stopped herself. *Wutt* would not do for the doll's name. She scrambled to think of something else.

"Wendy," she said. "It's Wendy."

"Can I hold her next?" a girl named Zara asked.

"And then me?" asked a preschooler named Ella.

That opened the floodgates. Many of the boys had already made their way back to the playground equipment, but most of the girls were entranced. They all clamored for a turn hugging the doll and reached for her hungrily, but before they accidentally caused damage with their overeager hands, Gabby hoisted Wutt safely onto her shoulders.

"Here's the deal," Gabby told the group. "Wendy is very special to me. You can *all* play with her, but it's very, very, *very* important that you don't poke any holes in her, or rip her apart in any way. You can hug her, you can throw her, you can love her up like crazy, but no holes and no rips. Understand?"

Gabby said it with her serious face, which all the kids

only saw in the most vital of times. They nodded solemnly, and Gabby gently lowered "Wendy" back to the ground. Immediately, Ella took one of the doll's hands, Bianca took the other, and they ran to the seesaw. Gabby thought she might have noticed Wendy's feet running along the ground with them, but she hoped if anyone else saw they'd chalk it up to a trick of the sunlight. Soon Wendy was sandwiched between Ella and Bianca on one side of the seesaw, while Zara and a boy named Scott took the other. For a second Gabby wondered if she'd done the right thing handing Wutt over to this group of strangers, but then she noticed "Wendy's" painted-on smile. It was twice as wide as it had been when the girl first changed form, and Gabby wondered if Wutt had ever had the chance to play freely with a group of kids her own age.

Scott's mom, Mrs. Lewis, frowned and checked her watch. "Gabby, it's the beginning of eighth period. Shouldn't you be with Maestro Jenkins in orchestra getting ready for the concert?"

In addition to Scott, Mrs. Lewis had an older son named Andrew, who was in orchestra with Gabby and Satchel. Gabby hated to lie to her, but there was no good way around it.

"Maestro Jenkins didn't want me over-rehearsed. He gave me the class time off so I could perform with more energy."

It was a semi-plausible lie, since Maestro Jenkins had

made offers like that in the past, but Mrs. Lewis still pursed her lips. "I love that you're here playing with the kids, but I'm assuming this isn't the kind of rest he had in mind. And I'm positive he wouldn't want your concert dress to look like that."

Gabby looked down at herself. Her white blouse was streaked with bright green grass stains and splotches of brown dirt, her knee-length black skirt was wrinkled and twisted the wrong way around her body, and her black tights were ripped at the knees. She lifted a hand to her face and could feel the layer of grime. She gave Mrs. Lewis an embarrassed smile. "I have a change of clothes at school. And I can clean up there, too."

"I hope so," Mrs. Lewis said. "After all, I'm sure you'll be playing solo. You need to make a good impression."

Gabby didn't have the heart to tell her that she wouldn't be at school until *after* the concert, when she'd deliver Wutt back to Edwina. She was thrilled when a moment later, Mrs. Lewis took Scott home to grab a snack before the concert. Now she wouldn't have to keep up appearances. She could concentrate on Wutt and on Ellerbee, who was still lurking in the trees. At some point she'd have to find a way past him, but so far she had no idea how.

In the meantime, the kids played with Wutt. From the seesaw, they all scrambled to the slide, and took turns going down with "Wendy" cuddled in their laps. Then they brought the doll with them for secret clubhouse meetings at the very top of the play structure and afterward gave her a turn getting her legs buried in the sandbox. They even strapped her into the baby swing and took turns pushing her as high as she could go.

Despite everything, Gabby felt warm and happy inside. Earlier in the day she'd thought the best thing she could do for Wutt was teach her about Earth through her school classes. Now Gabby understood she was giving the little girl something far more important—the experience of not just understanding Earth, but *belonging* on it.

The kids moved away from the playground equipment to play catch on the lawn. "Wendy" was the ball. Gabby imagined how free and fun it would be to soar through the air and not have to worry about hitting the ground. She could imagine Wutt's happy giggle with each toss and the comfort of landing in a pair of little hands. Or getting scooped up again after a tumble into the grass.

Gabby wasn't the only one charmed by the kids' games with Wutt. Several parents and nannies stopped their sideline conversations to watch the fun, and when the kids asked for a couple of grown-ups to throw Wutt, so the children could all stand between them for Monkey in the Middle, April's mom and Zara's dad eagerly volunteered. Zara's dad tossed

Wutt to April's mom, and all the kids leaped and squealed as they reached for the flying doll. The same thing when April's mom threw it back to Zara's dad.

"Throw her *far*, Daddy!" Zara shouted, and then all the kids joined in. "Yeah, throw her far!" "Make Wendy fly!" "Make her fly through air!"

"You really want to see her fly?" Zara's dad asked. He grinned at April's mom and waved for her to move back. She did, and the kids beamed eagerly as Zara's dad wound up to throw Wutt. Even Gabby was excited to see her friend soar across the field. Zara's dad cocked his arm back and threw . . .

. . . but he didn't know his own strength. Wutt soared not only high over the heads of the kids, but also over the head of April's mom. Wutt flew well beyond the woman's leaping reach, all the way toward a group of trees.

The group of trees. The one where Ellerbee was hiding in wait.

"NO!" Gabby wailed. She raced toward the still-soaring doll, but Wutt was on a beeline for Ellerbee. Long before Gabby was even close, the janitor stepped forward and held out his hands, eager to make the catch. He looked so hungry for success that Gabby could practically see him drool.

Suddenly, the roar of a motorcycle made everyone look up, but only Gabby died a little inside at what she saw.

Mr. Lau, his cape flying out behind him, rode the bike.

He zoomed toward Ellerbee, and without slowing for even a second, he stood on the foot pegs, reached one hand off the handlebars, and plucked Wutt from the air. In a single motion, he stuffed her into a large metal box on the side of the bike, then flicked a lock to seal her in.

"Ha-*ha*, old man!" he cried to Ellerbee as he zoomed away. "You lose—*I win!*"

"NO!" Ellerbee roared. He struggled to put on his Shoombas again so he could chase Mr. Lau, but Gabby didn't stick around to watch. She tore after Mr. Lau's motorcycle, pumping her arms and legs as hard as she could. When her dress shoes got in her way she kicked them off. She felt the bottoms of her tights give way until she was barefooted, sprinting over grass, dirt, and through clumps of brush. She ignored the pebbles and sticks that poked her feet, ignored the low branches that tore her tights and scratched her legs and arms. She ran long after the motorcycle was out of sight, ran toward the sound of its engine until even that was gone. She ran until every breath clawed its way into her throat, and when she finally stopped she bent double, her hands on her knees, gasping for air. Her lank curls hung in her face, damp with sweat.

Wutt was gone. Mr. Lau had taken her to Houghton. To a man who wanted to "eradicate" her. Gabby had thought she was a big hero, giving Wutt a real playdate with humans her own age, but all she'd done was give Wutt's enemies the chance to capture her . . . which they had.

Wutt had trusted Gabby. Wutt's parents and Edwina had trusted Gabby—trusted her with Wutt's *life*—and now the girl was gone. Gabby could see Wutt's face in front of her: the blue skin; big black eyes; red curls; toothless, trusting smile. She could feel Wutt's arms around her neck and the weight of her small body in her arms.

Gabby couldn't hold herself up anymore. She toppled onto the ground, curled her knees into her chest, and cried.

"Wutt?" a small voice asked.

A tiny hand touched Gabby's arm.

Wutt was back! She got away from Mr. Lau! An atomic blast of joy exploded inside Gabby, and she sat straight up, already beaming and ready to hug the girl close.

Except it wasn't Wutt. It was Evan, a two-year-old boy who had been at the playground. His nanny, Davida, crouched down behind him. Both Davida and Evan's faces scrunched with concern.

"What?" Evan asked again. "What wrong?"

"Are you okay, Gabby?" Davida asked. "Maybe I should call your mother."

Gabby couldn't explain this to her mother. Not yet. She needed time. "No, it's okay," she said. "It's just the doll. It was really important to me."

Davida nodded. "Yeah, that was strange what happened over there. We asked the Scottish guy about it, but he didn't say much. The other one . . . I'm afraid he's long gone."

The words clanged in Gabby's stomach. She nodded dully.

"Are you sure you don't want me to call your mom?" Davida offered again. "You're kind of . . . well, you're kind of a mess."

"I know," Gabby admitted. She tried to scrape the last of her mental energy for some kind of excuse, but came up empty. "I overreacted, I guess."

Davida smiled. "You're twelve, right? I remember twelve. It's the hormones coming in."

Gabby didn't have the strength to be mortified. She just nodded and let Davida help her up.

"You need a ride anywhere?" Davida asked. "I'm taking Evan home; I could drop you on the way."

Gabby knew Davida. Accepting a ride from her would be fine, but the only place Gabby wanted to go was some small, windowless room, far away in another country, with nothing in it but a giant bed with layers of comforters and a blanket with a silky edge. Then she could crawl in, rub the blankie edge on her cheek, and sleep for years and years and years until maybe she could forget everything that just happened.

She had a responsibility, though. She had to let Edwina know what happened. She had to admit her failure and face the consequences . . . which hopefully wouldn't include the entire planet being blown to bits.

"I need to go to school," Gabby said. "Can you take me there, please?"

chapter
THIRTEEN

the Brensville Middle School Orchestra performed in the Melchamp Auditorium, a large, stand-alone theater that sat right next to the school and rivaled the downtown home of the city's orchestra. Melchamp Auditorium was Gabby's favorite place in the world. Normally, just the sight of it made her happy, and on performance days she swelled with pride knowing she'd earned the privilege of playing in such a beautiful venue.

Yet today, when Gabby waved good-bye to Evan and Davida and looked at the auditorium, she felt hollowed out and miserable. She didn't deserve to play here. She didn't deserve anything.

She looked at her watch. Eighth period had ended ten minutes ago. The school day was over, and kids roamed the pavement in front of the school, talking in happy clumps. Some looked at Gabby, raising their eyebrows or laughing at her disheveled messiness, but Gabby barely noticed. She heard everyone as if through water, and they all felt far away from her.

"Gabby! Hey, Gabby!"

Andrew Lewis, Scott's older brother, was racing out of the middle school along with five other boys from orchestra. The whole group followed Andrew toward Gabby. They looked her up and down. "What happened to you?" Andrew asked.

He sounded interested, not judgey, but Gabby was too numb to give him an answer. She just shrugged, and Andrew left it at that. "Come in with us," he said. "Maestro Jenkins won't get mad at us for being late if we're with you."

Gabby hadn't planned on facing Maestro Jenkins. Edwina had said she'd meet Gabby in the auditorium after the concert, so Gabby had hoped to wait outside and catch her before she went in, or just slip in afterward once the crowd had left and find her then. Actually going backstage and explaining to Maestro Jenkins why she'd skipped orchestra and why she couldn't play in the concert . . . that wasn't on her agenda.

Still, when the boys surrounded her, she didn't have the energy to object. She let them herd her along through the backstage door and into the high-ceilinged chamber filled with all the ropes, pulleys, and lights that would make the stage come alive once the thick blue curtain was lifted.

"*O . . . M . . . G!*" Madison Murray whined in a voice so loud that anyone already in the audience must have heard it. "What is *wrong* with you?" She clip-clopped over in her shiny heels, and the small part of Gabby that was still paying attention noticed that Madison had indeed changed her clothes since lunchtime. This might have been her second-best skirt and blouse, but it was even frillier than her best one.

Once she reached Gabby's side, Madison took an exaggerated deep breath, then proclaimed, "Gabby Duran, you *reek!*"

Everyone turned, stared, and sniffed the air. Satchel, who had been drinking from a water bottle, actually did a spit take, spewing like a hose all over the backstage floor.

"Not the entrance I expected, Gabby." Maestro Jenkins's long, towering form strode backstage center. "Nor the look I expected, though as a rule I do support the creative eccentric."

As little as it mattered now, Gabby supposed she owed Maestro Jenkins some kind of explanation. "Maestro Jenkins, about orchestra period . . ."

"Patience, Gabby! I was about to get to that." Maestro Jenkins spread his arms and urged all the orchestra members into a close huddle. Satchel maneuvered his way next to Gabby and tried to catch her eye, but she felt too wretched to let herself connect with him.

"You are correct, though," Maestro Jenkins continued. "Everyone here noticed that you were not in our eighth period session today. However, I did not tell them why. I left that honor for you. Would you like to divulge the contents of the note I put in your locker at lunchtime?"

Gabby didn't understand. She hadn't been back to her locker since well before lunch. If Maestro Jenkins had left a note there, Gabby hadn't seen it.

"Actually," she said, "if you don't mind . . . would *you* please do the divulging?"

Maestro Jenkins smiled approvingly. "Losing your humble veneer, I see. Very well then, I'll share the accolades myself." He lifted his voice to address the whole group. "I told Gabby," he said, "that I happened to be walking to my office during fourth period when my ears were rewarded by an absolutely stunning version of tonight's solo emerging from a practice room. I peered through the window, and there was Ms. Gabby Duran, making utter magic. I slipped a note in her locker to tell her that as far as I was concerned she could do no better. I would take that as her final audition and leave it to Ms. Madison Murray to try to top it during eighth period. As for Ms. Duran, she could have the period free"—he sniffed down his nose at Gabby, a mix of disgusted and amused—"to do as she saw fit."

This information was clearly as new to Madison as it was to Gabby. Her eyes grew fierce and she opened her mouth as if to object, but then she cleared her throat and pulled herself tall. "Maestro Jenkins, may *I* divulge what happened in eighth period? When I performed the solo and received a standing ovation from the entire woodwind section and most of percussion except one extremely biased drummer?"

Satchel bumped his arm against Gabby's to let her know he was the extremely biased drummer in question. Gabby still couldn't meet his eye, but she gave him a wan half-smile.

"I believe you just did divulge, Madison," Maestro Jenkins said. "And indeed you gave a fine audition. Just not fine enough. Gabby Duran, I reward you this afternoon's solo! Now everyone get ready. House lights off in two minutes, then get to your places!"

Gabby dully registered calls of congratulations, as well as some arm squeezes, pats on the back, and one stomp on her toe from Madison that couldn't possibly have been accidental, but none of it sank in. She beelined for Maestro Jenkins.

"Maestro Jenkins," Gabby said, "thank you, but I can't do the solo this afternoon."

"Don't be ridiculous," Maestro Jenkins clipped. "You can and you will."

How could Gabby make him understand? She couldn't possibly play right now. She was empty inside. She had nothing to give the music.

Then she realized she had an excuse. "I don't have my instrument," she said.

It wasn't exactly a lie. Yes, her French horn was right next door in the cubby under her locker, but Gabby didn't have it *here*.

Maestro Jenkins looked at her like she was crazy. Then he pointed past her. "Gabby, your horn is on your chair, right where it's supposed to be."

Gabby turned. From here she could see out the wings to the stage. It was already set up for the orchestra, with the musicians' instruments sitting on their chairs or at their places. Maestro Jenkins was right. Gabby's horn was on her chair, exactly where it belonged. Satchel must have brought it over for her. Normally, she'd be thankful, but now her heart sank. Now she needed a new excuse.

"But Maestro Jenkins . . ." She tried to object, but the maestro shushed her and whisper-hissed to the entire orchestra, "House lights down now! Everyone to your places!"

He eyed Gabby and nodded for her to move. What could she do? It was dark with the house lights down, but glow-in-the-dark tape on the floor helped Gabby and the others shuffle successfully to their seats. By the time the house lights came up and the audience applauded, all the musicians and Maestro Jenkins were in place, the musicians standing next to their chairs.

Gabby saw her mom and Carmen in the front row, just like always. She forced a smile. If they noticed how disheveled she was, they didn't show it. Carmen clapped with great gravity, while Alice beamed and practically bounced in her seat.

Gabby shriveled inside. Her mom and sister seemed so proud of her. They had no idea how horrible she really was.

The applause died down as the orchestra sat. At a wave of Maestro Jenkins' baton, they moved their instruments to ready position and prepared to play.

For the first time ever, Gabby dreaded placing her French horn to her lips. She wasn't sure she could do it.

As if sensing her fear, the horn did the job itself. It leaned forward of its own volition and plooked its entire mouthpiece into Gabby's mouth.

She spluttered a little and pulled the horn away. The other horn players looked at her curiously. Gabby's horn silently tootled its valve levers, as if it was laughing, and Gabby quickly placed her hand over them, so it looked like she was making them move herself.

But she wasn't.

Hope tingled through her body and she leaned close to

the instrument. "Wutt?" she whispered.

The horn leaped up and down in Gabby's lap, and Gabby hugged it tight to stop the motion. She leaned over the instrument and whispered into its side. "But I don't understand. How did you—"

Gabby didn't finish her thought. Even though she hadn't been paying attention to Maestro Jenkins, Wutt apparently had. She pushed her mouthpiece against Gabby's lips just as the orchestra started to play, and Gabby instinctively dove in and played along. All Gabby's questions dissolved into the music, and everything but her overwhelming joy faded away as she and Wutt happily played song after song.

Then a spotlight shone on Gabby. The rest of the orchestra grew silent.

It was time for the final moment of the concert: Gabby's solo.

"Here we go, Wutt," Gabby whispered.

She rose, and a low murmur ran through the crowd. At first Gabby thought the audience was impressed with the way the spotlight glinted off Wutt's French horn body. The instrument almost seemed to glow.

Then Gabby remembered her ripped and stained clothes, matted hair, and dirt-smeared face. They'd been somewhat hidden by the rest of the orchestra at the beginning of the concert, but now they were in full view.

Gabby almost laughed. How she looked was the last thing she cared about right now. She gently placed her lips to the horn's mouthpiece and began to play.

The first time she and Wutt played this song, Gabby had been transported. She'd thought nothing could be as beautiful.

That performance was a pale ghost of this one.

From the first notes, Gabby and Wutt played a true duet. Wutt moved the valves not *for* Gabby, but *with* her, and each tone shift that came from Gabby moving her hand in and out of the bell held stronger and richer emotion. Though Gabby peeked at Maestro Jenkins and her sheet music, what she saw was every moment of her day with Wutt and how deeply she had connected with the little girl. Halfway through the solo, Gabby closed her eyes. She didn't need any more guidance. She and Wutt were in a musical world of their own, using the notes to tell their story in perfect unison.

When they finished, there was silence.

Then the whole audience burst into applause. Gabby heard the creaks and rustles as they rose to their feet. Even some of the other musicians stood and clapped, and Gabby laughed when she heard a hoot and turned to see Satchel doing a full-on celebration dance behind his drum kit. Maestro Jenkins himself gave her a small bow and a smile before waving his arms to guide the entire orchestra to their feet. The house lights came on, illuminating the audience, and Gabby beamed with glee at her mom and Carmen. Carmen nodded as she clapped, which for her was wild exuberance, and Alice screamed Gabby's name out loud. The orchestra bowed twice as a group, then Maestro Jenkins had Gabby step forward for a final solo bow. Instead, Gabby gestured to her French horn and leaned it forward—Wutt's own personal curtain call.

As everyone applauded, Gabby noticed someone else in the audience. A woman about halfway back, dressed all in black, with white hair pulled back in a severe bun. The seat to her left held two giant bouquets of roses. The bouquets seemed normal, though Gabby noticed the blooms seemed extra red. Almost unearthly so. And each bouquet trembled with what seemed like overwhelming emotion. Pride, maybe?

Gabby's heart jumped. The roses were Wutt's parents! They had to be! Wutt must have noticed them too, because the French horn let out an involuntary *BLATT* that should have been physically impossible without anyone blowing into it, but no one seemed to notice over the continued roar of the crowd. No one except Madison Murray, who opened her mouth in shock, then gave Gabby the stink eye.

Only as the curtain lowered, Gabby noticed the seat to Edwina's *right*. The man seated there was large and round . . . and wore a cape . . . and had a soul patch.

Mr. Lau.

Mr. Lau was with Edwina? And Wutt's parents?

Gabby wanted to see more, but the curtain came down all too quickly. Immediately, Gabby was swallowed by a maelstrom of congratulations. She hugged Wutt close and heard herself thank everyone, but her brain buzzed with such a wild mix of elation, relief, and confusion, she didn't even know what she said.

"That was *amazing*, Gabby!" Satchel said as he caught up to her and walked by her side. "Seriously amazing! I mean, I know you're always amazing, but this was like *amazo-*amazing! Like, *amazingly* amazo-amazing! Like—"

Gabby glanced around to make sure no one else was listening, then whispered, "Want to know *why* it was so amazing?"

She looked meaningfully at her French horn then smiled knowingly at Satchel. He plopped his hands over his ears, started humming, and strode away as fast as he could.

"Nice solo, Gabby," came another voice.

The compliment sliced across Gabby like a sword, and Madison leaned so close that Gabby could smell the peppermint from her breath spray. It smelled like evil.

"Thanks, Madison," Gabby said brightly. "No hard feelings?"

She stuck out her hand. Madison sneered down like she was more apt to spit in it than shake it.

"Feelings have nothing to do with it," she minty-hissed. "I *know* something's up, and I'm going to figure out what it is." She reached for Gabby's French horn, but Gabby turned and blocked the grasp.

"I have no idea what you mean," Gabby said innocently. "Great show, though!"

Gabby didn't wait for Madison's rebuttal. She hugged Wutt even closer and pushed her way out the backstage door into another throng of well-wishers. She smiled and nodded to all of them, but craned her neck and pushed through. She was looking for Edwina, but stopped when she found Carmen and Alice.

"Why isn't your horn in its case?" Carmen asked.

"*That's* the first thing you say to her?" Alice chided. "Gabby, you were incredible!"

"You were incredible in the concert," Carmen agreed. "You're also incredibly stinky. And why do you look like you were ground up in a food processor with our lawn?"

"Thank you," Gabby said. "And why do *you* look like you cut your own bangs with kids' scissors and a ruler?"

"Because I *did* cut my own bangs with kids' scissors and a ruler."

"*Exactly,*" Gabby said, then turned to her mom. "You really think it was good?"

"It was incredible, Gabby," Alice gushed. She wrapped

her arms around both Gabby and her horn and rocked them back and forth. "Truly, truly incredible."

"*I* heard your solo was so hot, it boiled tungsten!" Zee cried. She had been at Principal Tate's robotics club as she'd promised, but now ran over to throw her arm around Gabby in a congratulatory half hug. "That's really hot," she added. "Tungsten has a boiling point of 5,660 degrees Celsius. That's, like, around *ten thousand* degrees Fahrenheit."

"Melt-a-human-body-to-ash hot, is how I put it," Satchel noted as he joined them from the auditorium. "Which if you ask me, way easier to understand."

"I couldn't have done it without my fabulous French horn," Gabby pointed out with a knowing smile to Zee.

"It's a French horn solo," Carmen noted. "By definition you couldn't have played it without a French horn. You also can't have a pastrami sandwich without pastrami."

"Oh snap, I would love a pastrami sandwich right now," Satchel said.

"I was making an analogy," Carmen said. "I wasn't actually talking about—"

"I think I might have some pastrami in the fridge," Alice interrupted. "How about we all go back to our house and celebrate?"

"Think you might have some cake with that pastrami?" Zee wondered.

"Cake with pastrami?" Carmen gawped. "That would taste terrible."

"Pretty sure she meant one after the other, Car," Gabby said, but even as she spoke, she saw something out of the corner of her eye.

A limousine. It was parked halfway around the corner, almost out of sight among the trees, but it blinked its headlights as if sending a coded signal through the dusk.

"I'll be right back," Gabby said. "I, um . . . have to grab my horn case from the main building. It feels really *alien* to carry my horn without it."

Zee understood. She quickly engaged everyone in a conversation about the full snack lineup they should enjoy back at Gabby's house. Once they were all distracted, Gabby slipped away. She rounded the corner behind Brensville Middle School and saw Edwina. The old woman stood alone near the back end of the limousine.

"Edwina!" Gabby gushed. She placed her horn on the ground and threw her arms around Edwina, but the woman stood stiffly and didn't move a muscle to respond. It was like hugging a steel pole. Gabby quickly felt ridiculous and embarrassed. She let go and stepped back a few steps. "It's . . . um . . . good to see you."

"I'm sure," Edwina said, not-so-subtly brushing any traces of Gabby's touch from her shoulders and black suit jacket. "I have something for you."

She opened the back seat of the limousine and pulled out an item Gabby recognized instantly.

"My purple knapsack!" she cried, slipping it onto her shoulders. "But I thought it was—"

"Far aloft in the highest room of the Tower?" a voice boomed as Mr. Lau emerged from the limo. "Indeed it was, but once I had Wutt safely back to Miss Winnie here . . ."

He slung an arm around Edwina's shoulders. Edwina glared.

"I have access to Blichtencritch cringling acid that would dissolve you in two-point-one seconds," she said.

Mr. Lau removed his arm from her shoulders.

"As I was saying," he continued, "once Wutt was safe with *Edwina*, I retired to the place from whence I'd seen you and Ellerbee soar out the window and retrieved your misplaced item."

"I don't understand," Gabby said. She turned to Edwina. "I told you I thought Mr. Lau was from G.E.T. O.U.T. Why didn't you tell me he's with A.L.I.E.N.?"

"Because I'm not *with* A.L.I.E.N., my young friend," Lau answered. "I *am* an alien. From the planet Zeeliwhiz Five, in the Stradflarn System."

He took a deep bow, and Edwina tamped down an impatient sigh.

"He wasn't in our database," Edwina admitted. "Many still aren't."

"By choice!" Mr. Lau crowed. "Large registry systems rarely bode well in my experience. I fly under the radar as I ply my trade as a humble substitute teacher, but I pride myself on sussing out and befriending those secretly like me. You might say I have excellent *A*-dar."

"I might not," Edwina sniffed, then turned back to Gabby. "Though I will say that unbeknownst to myself, your Mr. Lau substituted last year for a second grade class that included a certain sluglike friend of ours."

Gabby thought about it, then lit up as she realized, "Philip? You know Philip?"

"Quite well, yes," Mr. Lau said. "And John and Lisa, who had been monumentally troubled over their inability to find a sitter. So when they met a young whelp named Gabby Duran, they told me. And when I saw that selfsame Gabby Duran would be in my math class at Brensville Middle School, I kept an eye on her. Then lo! You came into my class, and what to my wondering eyes did appear—"

"It's not *War and Peace*," Edwina snapped, then returned her focus to Gabby. "The man figured out Wutt's true nature, he'd heard the rumors about Houghton—"

"It's all the buzz on Spacebook," Lau interjected before Edwina silenced him with another glare.

"—and being on the inside at the school, he was able to peg Mr. Ellerbee as Houghton's man on the take."

"Indeed! But I played it up around Mr. Ellerbee like I was working for Houghton as well," Mr. Lau admitted. "That way he couldn't reveal my true identity to G.E.T. O.U.T."

The pieces were all falling into place now as Gabby played back her and Wutt's day in her mind. All except one.

"Okay," Gabby said. "So, Edwina, when you called me and said we had a bad connection, were you already in touch with Mr. Lau? And was that just your way of getting him some kind of GPS location on me?"

"Oh no, we truly did have a satellite out at the time and you were in terribly grave danger," Edwina said. "But you handled it beautifully, so thank you for that."

The French horn Gabby had placed next to her started bouncing up and down and tootling its valves.

"No, of course I didn't forget about you, Wutt," Edwina said. "And neither did they."

As she spoke, she peeled a pair of white silk gloves from her hands, then set them on the ground. Just as Gabby remembered that Edwina was bare-handed during the ovation, the gloves changed form. They sprouted into two small creatures, each one no higher than Edwina's knee. Both had giant liquidy-black eyes, paper cut nose slits, blue skin, and blue toothless mouths. The one on Edwina's right had long, flowing purple curls. The one on her left had short hair that was bright red.

"Wutt's mom and dad," Gabby breathed.

Wutt immediately popped back to her true form with a shriek so high and shrill it hurt Gabby's ears. The little girl raced to her parents, who sandwiched her in a huge hug. When she pulled away, the three of them spoke in rapid currents that sounded to Gabby like a buzzing hive of bees.

"Indeed," Edwina agreed, gesturing to one and then the other. "Her mother, Hoo, and her father, Ayedunno."

The two parents turned their massive eyes on Gabby, and she suddenly felt a chill. Would they be angry with her that Wutt had come so close to getting hurt on her watch? In unison the two moved closer, flanking her, their eyes unreadable. Together they nodded solemnly, and Gabby understood what they wanted. Nervously, she crouched low to the ground.

Both Hoo and Ayedunno threw their arms around Gabby for a tight hug, on which Wutt pounced, so she could join in. Gabby laughed and hugged them back.

"Wutt told them she had the most wonderful day of her life," Edwina said. "This is their way of thanking you."

"I got that." Gabby giggled. When they pulled back from the hug she added, "And I want to thank you, too. Wutt's very special. I'm really happy I got to know her and be her friend."

The three started buzz-talking again, but Edwina quickly cut them off. "Time for that on the way home. Let's go now." She unhooked a straight pin brooch stacked with simple beads from her lapel and held it out. "All right, Hoo's on first, Wutt's on second, Ayedunno on third."

The three aliens transformed into beads and strung themselves onto the brooch, which Edwina then hooked back onto her lapel.

"That'll do then," she said to Gabby. "Mr. Lau?"

Mr. Lau climbed into the limousine and Edwina was poised to do the same, but Gabby wasn't ready to let her go. Her mind was still reeling with questions. "Wait!" she said. "What about Mr. Lau? What happens to him? And what about Ellerbee? He's really not a bad man, he just—"

"Mr. Ellerbee has agreed to tell us everything he learned about Houghton," Edwina said, "and in return we'll settle him in a job he'll find much more satisfactory. Mr. Lau will go back to his regular life as a substitute."

"And Wutt? Will I get to babysit her again? Because I'd really like to. And G.E.T. O.U.T.—are they watching me now? Should I be looking over my shoulder? Like . . . I mean . . . should I be worried? Or could I be doing spy work for you between jobs? Because I would! I mean . . . assuming there will be another job ... Will there be another job?"

"We'll be in touch," Edwina said.

She slipped inside the limousine, pulling the door shut behind her. The engine started, and Gabby was sure it was about to drive away, but then the window lowered.

"It was a fine beginning, Associate 4118-25125A," Edwina said as the hint of a smile curled her thin lips. "You should be very proud. I am."

The window closed and the limousine rode away.

Gabby smiled.

A good beginning. That meant there'd be more. More aliens, more secrets, more danger.

Gabby couldn't wait.

Acknowledgments

We are beyond thrilled to present Gabby Duran to the world, and we know it never could have happened without the amazing efforts of so many people. First and foremost, we'd like to thank the amazing Jane Startz, for being the ultimate matchmaker and bringing the two of us together. Jane's vision is unparalleled, and we're honored to have her in our corner. Equal thanks to Kane Lee, for his always-insightful notes and excellent story sense. Together, Jane and Kane are a formidable team and Gabby's world would never have become what it is without them.

Next, we'd like to thank our incredible team at Hyperion. Our editor Emily Meehan had the vision to see everything Gabby could become, and we're so grateful she brought us under her wing. Together, Emily and Jessica Harriton are an editorial dream team. Their story notes were dead-on, and inspired us to dive eagerly and excitedly into each rewrite.

Thanks also to copyeditor Jody Corbett, who ran through the manuscript with a fine-toothed comb. She made sure we never contradicted ourselves in the details, and called us on all our verbal tics. Thanks to publicist Jamie Baker, for working so hard to tell the world about Gabby, and get her story onto everyone's radar. Finally, thanks to Marci Senders, whose eye-popping cover design made us squeal with glee in dolphin frequencies, then jump up and down and do a giant happy dance.

On a personal note, Elise would like to thank and hug and get all gushy over her husband Randy, daughter Madeline, and dog Jack for their unending love and support. She sends a huge thanks to Annette van Duren, her longtime and wonderful agent. She'd also love to thank all the rest of her friends and family individually... but that would take up way too much space. Instead she'll single out one: Sylvia Allen. Mom-Mom Sylvia, you make 98-years-old look GREAT!

Daryle would like to profusely thank Liz Lehmans and Jeannie Hayden for their long-term support of Gabby Duran in all of her many incarnations, and Jack Brummet and Keelin Curran for their help in making the Gabby project happen. She'd also like to thank Dan Elenbaas for the opportunity to create Gabby in the first place, and Farai Chideya for putting Gabby in Jane Startz' able hands. To Cynthia True, Erik Wiese and Marya Sea Kaminski, thanks for always helping with the tough decisions and giving your advice so generously.

Most of all, we want to thank YOU, our fabulous readers! We do the writing, but Gabby comes to life in your imaginations. Thanks for hanging with her, and we hope you'll join us for Book Two!

Much love,
Elise and Daryle